"The Pameroy mysteries never disappoint! I love how history gets mixed into the present. After reading this book, I really feel like I know Lillia and her Grauntie. Great read. Can't wait for the next!"

"What a fun mystery! I feel like I am right there with Lillia and Charlie during their adventures. Humorous, lighthearted and quite a page turner! I will definitely be recommending this one every chance I get!"

"Drawn into this book right from the beginning! My thirteen-year-old niece has read books in this series and loved them. So, it's been nice that we've both enjoyed and can chat about them! Great read not just for tweens."

"The Pameroy Mystery Series is such fun reading! I never figure out the ending until the last page. I can't wait to see what paranormal adventures will come next for Lillia and Grauntie!"

BROKEN CURSE

A PAMEROY MYSTERY IN ARIZONA

BRENDA FELBER

Cover design-eBook Launch

Publisher-Laughing Deer Press

Publisher's Cataloging-in-Publication data

Names: Felber, Brenda, author.

Title: Broken curse: a Pameroy mystery in arizona / Brenda Felber.

Series: Pameroy mystery.

Description: Schofield, WI: Laughing Deer Press, 2018.

Identifiers: ISBN 978-1-948064-05-7 (pbk.) | 978-1-948064-06-4 (ebook)

Summary: Lillia travels to the Superstition Mountains of Arizona. She helps her friend Sammie prove who set the fire at the Bender's horse stables.

Subjects: LCSH Superstition Mountains (Ariz.)--Fiction. | Cliff dwellings--Arizona—Juvenile fiction | Psychics--Juvenile fiction. | Friendship—Juvenile fiction. | Ghosts--Juvenile fiction. | Ghost stories. |

Mystery fiction. | Supernatural--Fiction. | BISAC JUVENILE FICTION / Mysteries & Detective Stories | JUVENILE FICTION / Horror & Ghost Stories | JUVENILE FICTION / Paranormal, Occult & Supernatural | JUVENILE FICTION / Historical / United States / 20th Century

Classification: LCC PZ7.F33375 Br 2019 | DDC [Fic]--dc23

ACKNOWLEDGEMENTS...

Broken Curse set in Arizona, is number eight in the series. Forty-two more state stories to go!

For this book, I was delighted to work with a new editor, Dana Osowski. I appreciate her abilities to tidy up my writing efforts!

I'd also like to extend a thank you to Jessica Kopecky Designs for my beautiful new logo. I love it!

To Bre Freund…the insights you shared provided me with a fresh look at the story and I thank you for helping me make it better! Plus, kudos to Grauntie Sharon for supporting your efforts.

Lastly, my gratitude for those family and friends who have supported, helped, and encouraged me along the way. I am forever grateful.

Now on to the mystery in Mackinac Island, Michigan.

CONTENTS

QUOTE TO PONDER...

"Don't try to comprehend with your mind. Your minds are very limited. Use your intuition."

Madeleine L'Engle (A Wrinkle in Time)

Dear readers,

Broken Curse is a fictional story, but it takes place in a real location! That rugged rock you see on the cover is the Superstition Mountain. It rises above the city of Apache Junction, just outside Phoenix, Arizona. Some places are believed to hold mysterious and unexplainable things… this is one of those places.

The cover image character is Sammie. She however, is not real. Some of the characters you'll read about are based on historical people. Elisha Reavis was a hermit living in the mountains and you can hike to the site of his ranch. Jacob Waltz was a miner called the Dutchman. Many gold hunters still search for his mine. If you go to my website you can see their images. Other characters are figments of my imagination, including Herbert Bender and his family.

I hope you get to visit the Superstition Museum and the Goldfield Ghost Town someday. Read the sign about the legends of the stone pillars as you look up at Superstition Mountain. Stop in at the white chapel which was used for a movie scene with Elvis Presley. Try the prickly pear fudge at Mother Lode Mercantile before strolling to the Mammoth Saloon for lunch or stopping at Miner's Grill for ice cream.

Drive the Apache Trail and see the remains of the

Salado cliff dwellings. But I don't imagine you'll see the spirits of the Indians who lived there like Lillia did!

I hope you enjoy exploring Arizona and a little of its history in *Broken Curse!* If you are lucky enough to live there or get to visit, I hope you'll send me a photo of yourself at one of the sites from the book. brenda@brendafelber.com

Happy reading…Brenda Felber

1

LILLIA

I stuck my head out the car window, grabbing my long hair to stop it from tangling in the warm Arizona wind. It felt wonderful to leave the snowy weather of Kansas.

The lights of Phoenix were left behind as we drove toward Apache Junction and the looming Superstition Mountain. What a strange name! The setting sun cast a purplish orange glow against the tall solid rock face. A pale moon globe rose in the deep blue sky behind it.

More and more of the tall cactus, with their people-like arms, appeared alongside the highway and up into the low hills. Such a different landscape than back home.

"Takes your breath away, doesn't it Lillia?" Grauntie Nora said from the front seat. "Who'd have thought such colors existed in the desert?"

"Kansas doesn't look like this at sunset."

"Still takes my breath away every day. I love showing our state to newbies," said Karen, the woman who picked us up at the airport. "Everyone seems to think Arizona is just rocks and sand and cactus."

Grauntie Nora laughed. "That was me, I'm ashamed to say. My mind is most definitely changing."

"Sorry I was late to the airport. I had something unexpected pop up and then all that Phoenix traffic to struggle through." Karen kept her eyes on the road as she let out a big happy sigh. "But this drive toward the mountains at sunset always calms me. The rains have been through and soon you'll see the desert come alive with colorful blooms."

"Blooms? In the desert? Do those tall cactus with the arms have flowers?" I asked.

"Yep," Karen said. "Those are saguaro cactus. They're not blooming for a couple of months though. But you'll see other cactus and wild flowers while you're here."

While we're here. I liked the sound of that. Loved Kansas, but the snow and winds had been especially bitter this year. I was glad to get these few days to escape with my grandaunt Nora. Our final destination was a friend's house at the base of the Superstition Mountain and we were almost there.

Closer to the mountains the air chilled. The rugged harshness of the mountain's face became clearer.

I remembered the words of our pilot come over the speakers as we flew across the Superstition Wilderness Area. "The Apache called these mountains, thrusting from the earth below us, the *Wee-kit-sour-ah*. Which in their language means *the rocks standing up*. Apaches believed their Thunder God lived there." His tone changed, getting lower, speaking slower. "I hesitate mentioning this, but many believe this Superstition Mountain Range harbors a curse. Hundreds of unexplained deaths have happened in the lands you see below you. Sometimes skeletons are found lying in..." Static broke up his announcement. All the passengers looked at each other as we listened to crackling spurts over the speaker system. Occasionally a word came through only to be swallowed up again. Suddenly his voice was back, loud and clear. "Oh thank goodness, we cleared that airspace. Now I can safely say, welcome to Phoenix. Once again, we are clear to land!"

The airline stewards began laughing and applauding. Soon all the passengers realized it was an act and joined in.

"Seriously though folks, be sure to visit Superstition Mountain and take a hike in the Superstition Wilderness." Then, in his ominous voice again he said, "Be careful though. Things are heating up this time of year."

2

THE CURSE

Superstition Mountain dominated the landscape here in Apache Junction. Most days Karen Bender felt it dominated her life too. Seeing the mountain every day was unavoidable. We all live in its shadow.

Karen had a love-hate relationship with the entire Superstition Mountains range. She believed they held a curse. After all, the Superstitions had taken the lives of her husband and his father. But she always ended with appreciation because they had also provided a livelihood for generations of the Bender family. Her son Matt ran the business his great granddaddy had started in the 1800s.

The Bender Stables offered tourists horseback riding out of the Goldfield Ghost Town area. Ever since it began, their main income came from taking people and supplies deep into the wilderness. Packing them in on horses and burros then guiding them into the depths of the mountains.

Early business had been with ranchers, miners, and explorers. Then after old Jacob Waltz died and word spread of his gold, more and more prospectors came. Now, much of the stable's income came from tourists and nature enthusiasts.

Lately Karen had been very disappointed in her son's business skills. Of course his wife Laura doesn't help the situation, Karen thought as she turned into Kitty's driveway.

"Oh my gosh," Grauntie said with a tone of awe in her voice. "Kitty never let on that she owned a place like this!"

"It is quite the home," Karen said. "She's done a great job with the place."

Up lighting softly lit the cactus and succulents amid the desert landscaping. Dim down lighting lit the drive and walkway to the front door. In the distance, above the long low roofline rose the Superstition Mountain still capturing the sunset's glow. Interior lights controlled by a security system had turned on and created a soft, welcoming warmth through the etched glass of the front door.

"Kitty indulges herself with creature comforts." Karen noted that the two visitors were quite impressed.

"Come on in the front door, I'll show you around," Karen said as she punched in the code to disarm the alarm and unlock the front door. "Here we go." Karen stepped inside to allow Nora and Lillia an open view across the great room, past the stone fireplace, though the glass wall, out across the patio, and over the pool. This breathtaking vista of the mountain left them speechless.

LILLIA

Wow! I couldn't believe my eyes. This was where Grauntie Nora and I would be staying? Thank you Kitty!

While Karen showed Grauntie Nora the things she'd need to know, I took my own little tour around the place. Beautifully framed photographs hung on the hallway walls. All of them seemed to be from this area...desert plants, rock formations, a lake with stone cliffs edging it, and Superstition Mountain. I peeked in and out of open doors. An office, a craft room, bathrooms, bedrooms, and even a room that looked like it was used only for gift wrapping.

Grauntie called, so I raced back to the front of the house.

"Let's get our luggage in. Karen has to be leaving."

After we'd gotten our things settled in bedrooms,

Karen said, "I've saved the best for last. Step out and I'll show the patio and pool area." She walked toward the tall windows across the back of the house and began pushing them sideways.

Wait, were those windows or doors? An opening in the window wall grew and grew. By the time she was done, the whole side of the room was open to the night air. How cool was that?

In the distance was the stark rock face of the Superstition Mountain with a big round moon rising behind it. Ahead of us the swimming pool shimmered and sparkled, both from soft underwater lighting and from the moon's reflection on its surface.

Grauntie gasped. "Whoa, what a backyard!"

"This is crazy! Grauntie, did Kitty tell you she had a mansion?" I asked.

"She didn't. Karen, do you know her well? We met Kitty in Concord, Massachusetts only a few times before she made the generous offer of using her home for a warm weather getaway."

"We've been neighbors for over thirty years. Kitty and her husband did very well in the construction business. Her life was turned upside down when her husband died. Soon after she looked for someone to help manage her home and I offered because I live nearby. She sounded so bubbly and happy again when she told me she was planning to stay for several months in Massachusetts."

As we stepped outside, Karen said, "The pool is heated year round so please take time during your stay to enjoy it. The whirlpool spa on that other end is wonderful to relax in."

"Oh my, I will enjoy that." Grauntie slipped off her flats to dip her toes in the water. Little bursts of flickering twinkles spiraled out. "Now this is luxurious and a perfect temperature."

The curtain of water spilling over the edge of rounded stones and into the pool, provided soothing gurgling, hypnotizing sounds. Large palm trees stood scattered in the yard. I was in an oasis in the middle of the Arizona desert.

A shout came out of the darkness. "Hello neighbors!"

"Oh good grief, the Schmidt's. Sorry. Hope they don't bother you while you're here. They're sweet people," Karen said in a low tone as she leaned in toward Grauntie. "But they always seem to pop up unexpectedly." She called back, "Hi Edgar, how's Dorothy been? Is her hip doing better?"

From the low stone wall bordering the back patio, a woman's voice answered, "I'm doing much better. Thank you for asking. Karen is that you?"

"Yes Dorothy. Kitty has some out-of-town guests for a few days. I'm just showing them around."

"Well cheers to you all," Edgar said before the sound of crystal glasses clinking together cut through the night air.

Grauntie called back, "Thanks!"

Karen said, "If you'll excuse me, I have to get back to figure out that issue at the stables. What are you two planning for tomorrow?"

"I know I want to have my morning coffee out here and watch the sun rise over the mountain. Would you like to join me since you're in the neighborhood?"

"Thank you Nora, I will take you up on that. I planned on checking in on you two in the morning to see how your first night went."

"Great! I'll be waiting out here with coffee."

"Sounds perfect. I'll bring cinnamon rolls."

After Karen left, Grauntie and I started jumping, squealing, and running around like little kids. We slipped into our swimsuits and dove into the refreshing pool water, as stars appeared overhead.

"Grauntie, I can't believe we're here. This will be so much fun!"

Moon shadows fell across the patio area from the tall palms. Their stiff, green fronds rustled in the warm, gentle breeze. A few yips and quick barks sounded in the distance.

"Sounds like the coyotes are out roaming around tonight," Grauntie said.

I would soon learn that there are more than coyotes roaming around these hills.

4

FIRST MORNING

Beams from the rising morning sun reached for the sky, fanning up behind the mountain. The desert warmed. Soon the snakes would slither out to bask in the sunshine and quail would scurry between the clusters of scrubby bushes.

Grauntie Nora always enjoyed rising at dawn. Karen had stopped in for coffee earlier and asked if Lillia would like to join her granddaughter Samantha on an overnight packing trip into the wilderness. Matt, Samantha's father, would be taking a group in on horseback and spending the first night with them.

She couldn't wait to tell Lillia about it. When would she wake up? Even the spicy aroma of warm cinnamon rolls hadn't lured her out. The swim last night must have made her sleep like a baby. Ah, here she is.

"Morning sleepy head," Grauntie Nora said as Lillia stumbled out to the patio rubbing her eyes.

Lillia plopped down in a cushioned chair, holding her hand up to cover a yawn. "Give me a minute. Let me wake up." She stretched her arms over her head. "Ahh... this sun feels wonderful."

"I have a suggestion for our first morning ice cream. Miner's Grill in Goldfield Ghost Town. Superstition Mountain Museum is right down the road from it. We can stop there too. Oh and just wait until you see the car we can use. A red convertible! It'll be a perfect day for a drive with the top down. You like the sun and wind in your hair so this'll be perfect."

Lillia held her palm up before laughing. "Hold on! You sure can string a bunch of ideas together quick but I can't listen that fast."

"Well the jest of it is...get dressed...morning ice cream awaits." Grauntie Nora decided to save the news about the camping trip for a little later.

Goldfield Ghost Town's wide earth-packed street was lined on both sides with old buildings representing a bygone era. The Miner's Grill and Ice Cream Parlor was ready and waiting for Nora and Lillia's tradition of having ice cream for breakfast on their first morning in a new place. Grauntie Nora ordered Peaches and Cream and

Lillia chose Pecan Caramel ice cream, both with fresh warm waffle cones.

They left Miner's to stroll the main street, enjoying their cold treats as they took in the activity of the ghost town. They peeked in the windows of the Justice of the Peace building with its jail and the gallows next door. Old, rusting mining equipment was displayed near the entrance to the Goldfield Mine Tour. Tourists panned for gold at Prospector's Place.

Mother Lode Mercantile tempted them with its sign advertising fudge. Passing all the other things in the eclectic shop, Lillia headed straight toward the candy area with its big blocks of fudge…from Sour Watermelon to Prickly Pear fudge. After Lillia chose Rocky Road and Peanut Butter Chocolate, they headed back outside to explore more of the ghost town.

Grauntie first noticed the Time after Time Photography studio. Sepia photographs of women with long satin dresses and feather boas, men in cowboy hats with pistols in hand, and children in prairie dresses and old pants with suspenders were on display in the windows.

"This looks like fun," Grauntie said. "To dress up in western gear for a photo. Want to do it Lillia?"

"Sure, but it looks like they're not open yet."

"Oh well, maybe later." Grauntie noticed the adjoining art gallery. It had the same wooden sidewalk in front of it and rough, gray plank siding. But the inside of the gallery, full vivid colors of nature photographs, from close-ups of flowering cactus to sunsets reflected against the mountains, stood in stark contrast.

"Can I help you," a young attractive woman said, offering a welcoming smile. She wore a white cotton shirt over faded denim jeans.

"Hi. We're just browsing. But I must say you have some beautiful photographs. Some of this photographer's work is displayed in the house we're staying at," Grauntie said.

"Oh? Thank you. So you're just visiting?"

"Yes, from Kansas."

"Are you the Pameroy's staying at Kitty's house by any chance?"

"Now how did you know that?" Grauntie asked.

"I have ESP," she said with a big grin. She extended her hand to Grauntie. "Just kidding. I'm Laura Bender, Karen's daughter-in-law. She mentioned you arrived last night."

"So this is your work? It's gorgeous. Really captures the beauty of Arizona."

"Why thank you. It's easy to find beauty here in the desert." Laura turned to Lillia. "I understand you'll be traveling into the Superstitions with Sammie tomorrow."

5

LILLIA

"I am?"

My confusion must have been obvious because Laura said, "You are Lillia Pameroy right?"

I nodded. "Who's Sammie?"

Grauntie hugged me. "I answered yes for my grand-niece, who was still sleeping this morning when Karen told me the idea."

Laura's hand flew up to her mouth. "Oh, I'm sorry to spoil the surprise!"

"Surprise? What are you talking about?"

"Lillia, you are invited along on an overnight horse-back camping trip into the Superstition Wilderness!"

"I am! Wow! When? Are you going Grauntie?"

"No, this old lady is not going along. But you will ride in with Sammie and her dad."

I elbowed Grauntie. "You didn't mention anything about it."

"Hmm…seems I remember someone complaining I talked too much? Let me think. Who was that?"

"Well, I was sleepy then," I said, ducking my head.

Grauntie didn't let up. "And, if I remember right, you said you couldn't get a word in edge-wise."

Laura watched us with a grin twitching at the corners of her mouth. "So Lillia, seems like you're up for going along?"

"Yes. Positively yes!"

"My family's business, the Bender Stables, offer services to get riders into remote sites in the wilderness. It's called packing in because we pack up horses and burros with gear that the campers need. So instead of people having to hike miles and miles in the heat, we take them in on horseback and then set them up at a camp-site. In this case Matt is planning on staying one night, then coming back out and returning later to pick the group up."

It was an easy decision for me. I missed horseback riding ever since my horse was released to roam free in South Dakota. "I'd love to go."

"And I know you can handle it. You rode so often on Wild Heart," Grauntie said.

"Sammie is thirteen, just a year older than you, and

she's excited to have a traveling buddy with her. Matt is taking in a small group of writers who want a little inspirational retreat at Reavis Ranch. Spend a few days contemplating life in the wilderness I guess. I'd rather enjoy it and record it through my camera lense, but hey whatever floats your boat," Laura said with a chuckle.

"The full moon tomorrow night will be great for camping," Grauntie said.

"Speaking of a full moon, could I come over and do a shoot tomorrow night at Kitty's house? The moon will be unusually close to the earth. Kitty's patio is the perfect spot to set up."

"Of course, it would be fun to watch you work!" Grauntie said. "So when will we meet Sammie?"

"She's up behind the Mammoth Saloon helping set up horses for a trail ride. Maybe you could catch her there."

"Come on Grauntie, let's try to find Sammie," I said. Horses and camping! Woot!

The Mammoth Saloon's porch wrapped its exterior. Signs advertising cold beer and hot food hung on the large building. Country music poured out of speakers.

We walked through the dining area, already busy with tourists, and found our way to the back parking area. Horses were tied up to a railing. A long white trailer with small windows along its side was hooked up to an old pickup truck.

"That must be Sammie," I said, pointing to a tall lanky girl who was helping unload the horses from the trailer.

"They seem busy. I hate to interrupt them." Grauntie said.

Sammie's cowboy hat shaded her from the hot sun. A long braid hung down against her back. Her dusty cowboy boots were the real thing, no glittery ones like girls at school wear. Her worn jeans were tucked into the top of her boots.

I watched as people milled about, taking photos on their cell phones. Out of the corner of my eye, I saw a flash. Like something thrown toward the trailer. Next thing I knew, one of the horses coming out the trailer reared up, almost taking Sammie along into the air. The horse snorted and stomped her hooves sharply on the metal ramp before rearing up again, wildly pawing the air with her front hooves.

Heads snapped around at the sharp metallic sound and loud neighing. They stared wide-eyed as Sammie sprang into action, holding the frightened horse's reins short up against the bridle. She got it off the metal ramp and moved to one side. Still holding her short, she led the horse in small circles, continually murmuring and stroking her neck.

A man dressed in cowboy gear, confirmed Sammie was okay before getting back to the nervous looking riders. "Hi all, I'm Rex and hope you enjoyed that little performance. We want you to experience riding a true mustang into the wild land of the Superstitions. But seriously, our horses are well-behaved and trained. However, they are still large animals so we need to make sure you sign those release forms." His attempt at a joke to lighten the moment fell flat. No one smiled.

I watched as Sammie and her horse joined him. "This pony is mine, and she just wanted to let me know that she's ready and raring to go! Aren't you Dolly?" The tall horse flicked her nose in the air, her brown coat gleaming in the sunshine.

Some uncomfortable laughter from the waiting riders followed her comments. Rex added, "Sammie here is the best young wrangler in these parts. You're in good hands with her."

6

MEETING MATT

Sammie was shocked that Dolly would behave like that. She had been taken on and off these trailers her whole life. What caused her to suddenly rear up?

Matt saw the incident too. That sure was odd he thought. But then a lot of mysterious things have been happening lately. Was the curse of the Superstition Mountains hitting the family again? First the loss of Grandpa, then just a few years ago Dad disappearing. Now the stables seem to be getting hit with a string of unusual things. A horse randomly rearing up wouldn't raise a red flag, but when it was one in a line of such happenings, it made a man think.

Glad Sammie kept her wits and settled the horse down Matt thought. Stuff like this isn't something you want happening in front of a bunch of inexperienced people waiting to take a trail ride. Makes them nervous and the horses, sensing that fear, don't respond to the riders as well. Everyone signs a waiver with all the legalese on it about releasing us of liability, but sometimes those aren't worth the paper they're written on.

Matt walked up to his daughter as she put her foot in the stirrup and swung herself up into the saddle. "Did you see what startled Dolly?" Matt whispered as he leaned in and pretended to check the cinch on the saddle.

"Nope, I didn't Dad. That's not like Dolly at all."

"Hmm. Okay…well guess we'll never know. Glad you're riding her in the back of the line though. The riders will forget about it once you get out on the trail."

Sammie said, "Bye Dad. See you in an hour." She gently pulled the reins against Dolly's neck, turning her to join the line of waiting riders. She gave an all's ready whistle signal to Rex who waited in the lead position.

Matt watched the group start out toward Superstition Mountain and said a little prayer for their safe return, as he always did, before turning to close up the ramp. He didn't notice the man who'd slipped away from the side of the trailer, but he stopped when someone called his name.

He searched across the lot, before he saw a woman with her graying hair piled atop her head waving at him. Next to her stood a girl about Sammie's age. He approached them and said, "Howdy. Can I help you with something?"

"You're Matt Bender? I'm Nora Pameroy and this is my grandniece Lillia. We wanted to introduce ourselves to you and Sammie but didn't want to get in the way, especially after her horse got startled."

"Yeah, sorry about that. Dolly's not one to spook easily. Did you want to book a trail ride? We start another one around two o'clock."

"Oh no, though I'm sure that would be lovely," Nora said. "We understand you have invited Lillia along on a trip tomorrow."

Matt slapped the side of his head. "Oh sorry, I didn't put it together right away. You're the visitors from Kansas?"

Nora nodded. "Yes we are."

"Welcome to warm Arizona! Glad you got the chance to get away from the snow and cold. Sammie is so excited to have someone her own age along."

"I'm excited too Mr. Bender. I used to have a special horse in the Black Hills and we'd ride a lot there. But Wild Heart is running free now, so I don't get to ride as much," Lillia said.

"Is she at the Black Hills Wild Horse Sanctuary?"

"She is. How do you know about that?"

"We have a lot of wild horses around here and sometimes the herd needs culling. The sanctuary often helps with that."

Nora said, "Are the wild horses nearby?"

"Not right here in Apache Junction, but close. They're called the Salt River herd and they move around in several areas in the Tonto National Forest and across the Superstition Wilderness area. It's over 160,000 acres so they have room to roam. We try to control the population, but there still is a need for reserves or sanctuaries like Dayton Hyde founded in South Dakota. With Phoenix development sprawling and filling in available land, we are lucky to have big, open wild areas set aside."

When one of the stablehands let Matt know he needed to finish chores back at the stable, Matt said, "I'll see you two bright and early tomorrow morning at our stables. Happy to have you traveling with us."

7

LILLIA

I decided I should tell him what I'd seen. "Ah, excuse me Mr. Bender, one more thing."

"Sure, what is it?"

"I think I saw what caused that horse to startle and rear up. Out of the corner of my eye I saw someone who was standing behind the other horse trailer throw something toward Dolly."

"What? You're kidding." Matt looked around as though the person might still be there. Shaking his head he said, "I'll be darned. Who would do something like that? Thanks for telling me about it. I just knew Dolly wouldn't act like that for no reason."

People were leaving the area. "Do you think any of them might have caught a photograph of him?"

"So it's a man?"

"It happened so quickly, but I think was dressed like a cowboy."

Matt laughed and pointed out the stablehands he had helping him. "Like those guys?"

My cheeks flushed. "Oops, guess that's not much to go on, huh?"

Grauntie pulled me against her and playfully rubbed the top of my head. "Lillia has a bit of a detective in her. She likes to solve mysteries."

"Well I like a good mystery too. But this was probably one of the guys throwing a rope up into the truck. Or it could be just a big old horse fly biting her once too often. But I appreciate you letting me know that because we've had some unusual occurrences recently. I will have to start keeping track of them the way it's going!"

"Come on Lillia, let Matt get back to work. And we're heading to the museum. See you tomorrow."

"Tell Florence in the museum bookstore that Matt says hi and to take good care of you. The place carries lots of books about this area. My great-grandfather wrote several of them."

Grauntie Nora said, "We'll be sure to check those out. I love reading books about the areas we visit. Did he write one about the famous Lost Dutchman Gold Mine?"

"Yes ma'm he did. In fact, old Herbert knew the Dutchman."

My ears perked up when I heard about a lost gold mine. My brother Charlie would love that. He's all about maps and treasure hunting. "Who's the Dutchman?"

"He's one of the most legendary characters of the Superstitions. His name was Jacob Waltz, but Dutch is a common American term for someone of German descent. Stories grew that he'd found a bunch of gold up there," Matt pointed toward the mountains in the distance. "People have been trying to find where his gold came from ever since he died."

"Did they ever find it?"

"Nope, not yet anyway. Many have lost their lives looking for it though. So the legend of the mine and the curse of the Superstition Mountains keep growing."

I said, "Our pilot told us about a curse. So it's true?"

A flash of sadness crossed Mr. Bender's face.

"That curse is a legend, like the lost mine. Good question…are legends true? There's enough truth in them to keep the stories being told. I don't think deep down inside, the gold hunters expect to find anything. But they like the idea of the dream, the chance to plan a trip, study the old maps, and explore the area. Those things make it worth it to them. But don't get me wrong. If they found the gold, they wouldn't leave it behind."

"But what about the curse Mr. Bender? Is it true or not?"

"Ah, the curse. That's a story for another time," he said.

8

ORSON

Another day at the Goldfield Ghost town was in full swing. Tourists were pouring in from the parking lot just off the road. A tall, handsome cowboy stood near the old church at the top of the Goldfield hill taking it all in. Many of the men around here wore cowboy hats and boots. But if one looked closer, they'd notice that this man's hat was new, his cowboy boots shined, and his mustache perfectly groomed.

Such an idyllic scene he mused. People experiencing horseback riding. An old mining town coming to life. People out and about enjoying themselves with their families and friends. Goldfield Ghost Town did a good job of creating the illusion of a wild west town full of prospectors looking for gold and ranch hands coming in for a cold beer. Tourists being fake hung by the sheriff.

Cowboys pretending to die, shot in a gunfight performance.

Fake...illusions...all in good fun. He chuckled, just the way he loved it.

The startled horse scene was but a small pebble dropped in the big pond of life. Another set of ripples meant to put Matt Bender off his stride. He chuckled. Soon enough my legend will bring me fame and fortune. Patience Orson, patience.

He fought against the bile rising from his stomach. Little Matt taking over the family business. The business built by the sweat of his ancestors. Matt is nothing like his grandfather or his father before him. Those were real men. Rugged men.

He looked up at the mountain and shook his fist. You claim bodies to feed the legend of the curse. Give me some of that notoriety you possess. Some of the fame. I deserve it!

He let out a low sound. Not a chuckle. Not a laugh. More of an animal sound...almost a growl. Stop it Orson! You must control yourself. It should be soon. They will recognize your value.

He turned his stare toward the parking lot beyond, noticing the two who had been talking with Matt leave in a red convertible. Why had they pointed at the spot he'd thrown the rock from? Had they seen him?

His eyes followed them. They're driving toward the museum. Perhaps it is time I visit there as well, he mused. Make certain my books are displayed front and center as they should be.

The red convertible passed the black cutout silhouette of a prospector leading his burro packed with gear and into the small parking area at the Superstition Mountain Museum.

A one story building with shaded porches welcomed visitors. Small groups eating lunch occupied the picnic tables. The museum grounds sprawled out from the parking lot. Visitors strolled pebbly brown paths that wound away between old wooden buildings and up toward a large weathered barn with the words *Apacheland* clearly visible.

"Is this all real? It looks like a movie set," Lillia said.

Grauntie Nora said. "I understand that many of these buildings were moved here from an abandoned movie set, like that little white chapel and the Wells Fargo building. But let's start in the bookstore and interior museum first. We can walk around outside afterward."

The shop was bustling with people. It's shelves and cases filled with books, turquoise jewelry, colorful hand woven blankets, and souvenir items. Grauntie found Florence behind the jewelry display case. "We just left Matt Bender up in Goldfield. He said to say hello to you."

"Well bless his heart. He's such a sweet man. We keep hoping he'll write a book like his great-granddaddy did," Florence said with a wink.

"Could you show me those?" Grauntie Nora said.

"Certainly. Follow me." Florence led Nora and Lillia to cases full of books about the area. "Here are the ones he wrote. And let me suggest a few others for you if I may. I can hold on to them while you visit the museum right through that door."

9

LILLIA

As soon as I walked through the door and into the museum from the gift shop, I saw the display of stuffed animals. These weren't cuddly cute teddy bears, they were real animals…once upon a time…not anymore.

It mesmerized Grauntie Nora too. "Just look how they mounted that mountain lion. Like he's standing up to fight off the mountain goat."

"That's creepy. Why would anyone do that?"

"Do what Lillia?" But before I could answer she said, "Now there's one we don't see much, a javelina or peccary. Like a wild pig. Aww! Look at the cute little coyote."

"Stop…someone killed them and stuffed them."

"It's called taxidermy. And I doubt they killed them. Probably found them dead and preserved them. Oh look, there's the Lost Dutchman display." Grauntie's focus shifted, and she hurried off.

My attention returned to an object hanging on the wall of the animal display. It was long and flat, pretty pattern markings spread across it. What was that? Ew…a rattle snake! Don't want to meet one of those.

Grauntie waved me over. "Lillia, come look. Maps drawn to find the Lost Dutchman Gold Mine. Your brother would love these! Remember that silly little pretend Captain Jack's treasure map he got on the pirate cruise?"

"I do. Charlie actually went with it into the backwaters of the Bon Secour River to find treasure." I shivered, remembering the final outcome. I had to convince the ghost of an angry Pirate Queen that the treasure she guarded, wasn't really there. That was a scary scene!

Grauntie took a picture of the maps with her cell phone. "I'm going to send him a photo."

I took in all the various maps hanging in frames on the museum wall. "Look they call this one the Peralta map. It says they were a Spanish family that owned a mine here in the Superstition Mountains and it's believed they were chased out by the Apache. This one belonged to Julia Thomas. Wonder who she was?"

A tall handsome cowboy with a gray handlebar mustache walked up and said, "Julia Thomas was the kind soul who cared for Jacob Waltz on his deathbed. He left her that map as a way to repay her. She tried to find the site of the old Dutchman's gold, but never succeeded."

Grauntie said, "You seem to know a great deal about all of this."

"I've written several books on the subject and have a bit of the Lost Dutchman mine fever in me myself. I'm Orson. And you are?"

"I'm Nora Pameroy and this is my grandniece Lillia."

"Now don't go teasing an old cowboy like me. You aren't old enough to have a grandniece," Orson said.

I watched Grauntie blush. "You're an author? I just bought several books that Florence is holding for me. Would you please autograph yours for me?" Grauntie's words were tripping over themselves trying to get out of her mouth. "This is so exciting. Isn't this exciting Lillia? A real author right here. And like our own museum tour guide?"

"You're new in town?"

"Just visiting for a few days. We're from Kansas. A friend is letting us stay in her house. Do you know Kitty? No, you won't know her. What am I saying?"

Orson chuckled. "Now ma'm I believe I do. She lives near a friend of mine, Karen Bender."

"No? You know Karen!" I watched as Grauntie

looked up at Orson, her eyes all melty. I could hardly keep from laughing.

10

MANIPULATION

Orson almost felt guilty at the way he manipulated this old gal. "Karen is a lovely lady. She's a big part of our community here. I completed a great deal of research using some of her family archives. She was most gracious during that process. May I show you a few more of the artifacts here?"

"I'd enjoy that very much."

"Right this way Nora. I'll show you a piece made from the gold that Jacob Waltz left to Julia Thomas."

"He left her a map and actual gold as well?" Nora asked.

They walked together to another display case where, under glass, a small slim silver edged case rested on a blue velvet cloth. "Do you see the gold veins in the stone inlay of this matchbox?" Orson asked as he rested his hand on Grauntie's back and they leaned in closer.

"I do," she mumbled breathlessly.

"And see the small sign? It reads that they made this from the ore found under his bed, the gold he left to Julia."

"Oh my goodness. Thank you for showing me this. I might have missed it." Nora turned and looked for Lillia, but she was still by the Dutchman map display. "I must point it out to her. Looks like she's enthralled with Jacob and his legendary status. Tell me more about your research and writing please."

Orson didn't want to waste more time here, but he took a few moments to talk to the old gal before asking her, "I remember seeing a classy looking lady like you this morning up behind the Mammoth Salon. Were you making plans for a trail ride later?"

Nora giggled. "Oh no. We were there to meet Samantha Bender, but we missed her. My grandniece will be going with her on a trip tomorrow into the mountains."

Orson's this-is-interesting radar pinged. It might be a chance to make more mischief. "Is that the writers group? I encountered some of them in the local diner yesterday."

"Why yes, that's what Laura said." Nora's hand flew to her mouth. "Are you one of the group?"

Orson had to think quickly. This might be a good opportunity. He told the first lie that came to him. "They asked me to consider joining them to share my experiences as a published author."

"That would be so generous of you." Nora said.

11

LILLIA

I lingered longer by the Lost Dutchman display. That whole syrupy scene with Orson and Grauntie was too much for me.

"Hope you enjoy your visit here Lillia."

I spun around. Who said that? No one was near me. An elderly couple stood by the early farmhouse display, exclaiming over the cast-iron stove and old stoneware. Back at the animal display a young mother was pulling her toddler back from trying to get in under the rope to pet the big kitty. A teenager with thick glasses was looking at the geological exhibit, leaning over as if to read every sign.

Hmm...? Voices in my head I guess. Grauntie and Orson moved toward the museum exit door. She seemed to be looking around for me, so I started toward them, passing the teenager by the mineral display.

"Excuse me," he said. "You are Lillia, right?"

He caught me by surprise. Maybe I hadn't been imagining the voice. "Yes. Do I know you?"

He looked nervous as he pushed his glasses back up his nose with one finger. "No, but I'm your ghost guide. No, no. That's not right. I'm your spirit helper. No. Darn. What did they call me?"

"Spirit guide?" I asked.

"Yes that's it!"

"And you're here to help me?"

He considered the question before saying, "I am, but I don't know what I'm supposed to do. So I thought I'd check in with you. Is there anything you need?" He seemed to stand up straighter as if he'd gained confidence in his position.

This nerdy looking teenager was my spirit guide? Not like any of the others I'd had. "Ah, I don't think so." I almost felt sorry for the guy. He seemed out of his element here.

"Well okay then." He looked around trying to assess what should happen next.

"Is anything wrong?"

His shoulders sagged. "To be honest, I'm new at this guide stuff. Suppose you can tell, huh?"

He seemed kind of sweet. "I understand confusion, happens to me all the time. But things are nice and quiet so far…might be an uneventful trip for once. Thanks for showing up though. Nice to meet you."

He looked relieved and let out a sigh. "See you around Lillia. Well ah, I mean nice to meet you too. Gosh I'm not sure what I mean. Guess I'll check out the Native American display now. Bye."

"Bye."

I caught up with Grauntie just in time to hear Orson say, "Perhaps I'll see you again?"

Did he actually wink at her? Ugh!

"Enjoy the rest of your stay ladies."

Grauntie said, "Please don't forget to sign your book. I'm sure it must be one of the ones Florence recommended."

"Will do," Orson said.

After we finished in the museum, we returned to the bookstore.

Grauntie searched for the book Orson signed. "Florence I'm so embarrassed, I asked a man in the museum, Orson somebody, to autograph his book for me. But looks like I didn't purchase one of his."

"He stopped to ask me about it. To be honest Nora, he's not our staff's favorite writer. We rarely recommend his books."

"Oh dear, now I feel foolish. I can still purchase one though? If I run into him somewhere, I could still get his autograph," Grauntie Nora said. "He was so handsome."

Florence reached down to the bottom bookshelf, moving aside a few other books, to pull out the one she was looking for. "Here you go Nora."

My teenage guide walked by us, giving me an awkward hip-height hand wave as he faded out of sight.

Now the sun blazed down from a clear blue sky. Museum visitors moved from shady spot to shady spot and baby stroller sun shields popped open. Above it all Superstition Mountain loomed, wavering in the heat.

I encountered a sign on the path that explained the legend of the stone pinnacles on top of Superstition Mountain. Both the Pima and the Apache told stories about a great flood that angry gods sent to punish the sinful people of their tribes. It read that many struggled to get up on top of the big mountain to save themselves, but they were turned to stone.

Grauntie looked toward the mountain, shading her eyes with one hand. "Stone Indian maidens…hmm? That's an interesting image. Makes the mountain feel even more distant and strange. It sends off a vibe, like it has a life of its own."

My thoughts exactly.

12

BURRITO THE BURRO

Tiny particles of dry earth rose from the ground as visitors walked the paths, peering in the windows of the old-time jail and posing for photographs with a team of horses hitched to a red stagecoach.

An old man stood next to a fully loaded burro. He posed for photographs with tourists too, always with a smile on his face. Jake's role here was as the legendary Jacob Waltz of the Lost Dutchman Mine fame. He stroked his bushy gray beard, remembering his days as a movie actor in the western shows filmed in Arizona. Heck, he even met Elvis Presley when he made that movie Charro.

Burrito pushed her warm hairy nose into Jake's tummy as if to ask are we done here yet? Jake rubbed the rough ridge of hair along the burro's neck. His buddy for over twenty years, through countless parades and hundreds of kids sitting on her back for photos.

A small crowd was gathering now as Jake took on the persona of the Lost Dutchman to entertain the curious crowd. "I'm Jacob Waltz and this here is Burrito. She's been my trusty companion as I travel into the Superstition Mountains in search of gold. Donkeys and burros were first introduced to North America by Spanish conquistadors. They were valued for their ability to carry large loads over Mexico's difficult terrain. The word burrito means little donkey in Spanish. Now I imagine most of you think of the Mexican burrito only as a delicious food. Am I right?"

The crowd gathering around him laughed, and the children jumped up and down shouting out yes.

"Well the burrito and the burro have something in common. Both can hold a lot of stuff! Isn't that right?" He took Burrito's cute face in his hands and lifted it up. On cue she let out a heehaw, bringing another laugh from the gathering crowd.

"She agrees! Burrito and I would be happy to pose for photos," he said.

"Come on Lillia, let's get a picture with him," Grauntie said.

As the small group pushed forward to pose with Jake and Burrito, a fancy white pickup truck drove slowly out of the parking lot nearby. "Look, there's that hottie Orson."

"Grauntie!" Lillia exclaimed.

With fake shock on her face Grauntie held up her hands. "Just a spontaneous reaction."

"I'm glad you didn't chase his truck for an autograph."

"Hey there smartie pants. I'm not that far gone," Grauntie said.

Jake overheard the woman mention Orson. That character sure could turn the ladies heads he thought. Too bad they didn't understand there wasn't much more to the man.

Lillia never got a photo with Jake because a call from Karen interrupted Grauntie Nora. She was asking about getting together with Sammie tonight.

In the meantime, Jake and Burrito were busy with other tourists.

13

LILLIA

Back at Kitty's house, I had just changed into my swimming suit when Karen and Sammie walked through the gate and up our driveway.

Grauntie opened the front door with her usual flourish. "I'm so glad you agreed to join us tonight."

When she saw me in my swimsuit, Karen said, "Oh sorry Sammie I forgot to remind you to bring a swimsuit!"

Sammie's face fell, then brightened up as she said, "Didn't I leave one at your house once Grandma? I'll run back and get it."

Karen quickly added, "Lillia, want to go with her?"

I grabbed one of the big beach towels to wrap around me and flip flops for my feet. As we walked along the rough gravel street Sammie said, "Heard I missed seeing you earlier today. It'll be so fun having you along on our packing trip tomorrow."

"I saw you loading up horses and how that one reared up. I was scared for you."

"That's my horse Dolly. She's never like that," Sammie said as she shrugged her shoulders. "Something must have startled her, but I can't imagine what."

Even though her dad thought what I saw was no big deal, I decided to mention it again. "Ah Sammie, I might have seen what startled Dolly."

"Really? What did you see?"

"I noticed a flash of someone throwing something and then slipping away. Not running, more like a fast slinking."

"Seriously?" Sammie stopped walking. "I had a funny sense this morning. Do you ever get those?"

"For sure." I knew what she meant. I don't how many times that's happened to me and I've learned to trust it. "I mentioned it to your dad when Grauntie and I met him after you all left on the trail ride."

"What kind of name is Grauntie, anyway?"

"She's my grandpa's sister. I kinda smushed grandaunt and great-aunt together."

"I like it!"

"Anyway, your dad brushed off what I told him."

"Sorry Dad didn't believe you. He's been super busy and was probably distracted."

"That's okay. My only identifying feature was the guy being dressed like a cowboy."

Sammie's smile started in her eyes before she let out a little snort. "Too funny. I can just picture Dad pointing out all the cowboy hats and boots on the guys around there. But thanks for telling me too Lillia. Been some troubles at the stable and they seem to be getting worse. It's all little stuff but it's adding up. Be right back out."

Sammie ran toward the front door of a modest Spanish style home across the street. Its rough textured walls were painted the color of the surrounding desert. The roof had those strange looking rounded orange tiles. A tree with gray-green bark, a sharp branched shrub, and three small cactus clustered in the front yard. Water trickled from a colorful Mexican clay pot fountain sitting in the shaded entry.

Sammie ran back out, swimsuit in hand. "Found it. Come on friend, let's hit that pool."

We were in the pool within two minutes after getting back. The neighbors from next door came over and I heard bits of their conversation with Karen and Grauntie, plus lots of laughter.

Sammie and I hung out in the pool. The water was

just the right temperature as the evening air cooled and the moon rose over the mountain.

Lying on our pool floats we stared up at the stars and tried naming the constellations. About the only one I knew was the Big Dipper. But Sammie showed me it was part of Ursa Major, or Great Bear.

"Can you see the Little Dipper too?" Sammie floated by.

I tried, but she had to help me. "Okay, I see it now. And isn't that bright one the North Star?"

"Yep," Sammie said from somewhere across the pool. "That's part of the Little Bear constellation. Or otherwise known as Ursa Minor."

As I floated along amazed at seeing more and more stars appearing overhead, I saw Karen standing at the edge of the pool. "Sammie's good at sky gazing and identifying the stars, but it's time to head home now. You two have to be up early in the morning."

14

BENDER STABLES

Meanwhile, in the office of Bender Stables, Matt sat at the scarred wooden desk that had been used by generations of his family. His great-grandfather Herbert Bender left the busy hustle and bustle of the East coast behind one fine spring day in 1846. He spent a couple of years in St. Louis working on the riverboats. When stories about the goldfields in northern California came back from scouts passing through, he set off again. A year later, he left California for Arizona with a few gold nuggets in his pockets and a beaming bride at his side.

Arriving in Arizona in 1851, Herbert still possessed the desire to find gold. His first child was on the way and that meant staying closer to home. No more months away at a mining camp. His wife loved the low foothills at the edge of the mountain wilderness near the small town of Phoenix. He staked a piece of land and built a modest home to shelter his growing family.

Herbert established a stop for the stage coaches needing to rest their horses. It grew into a business supplying horses, mules, and burros for miners and ranchers. Meeting old Jacob Waltz was the beginning of a powerful restlessness once again. The lure of the mountains and the elusive gold won. He left his family for days to pursue his dreams in the wilderness, while his young bride kept the stables running and prayed for his safe return from the dangerous wild lands.

Matt stretched his arms over his head and tipped back in the wooden rolling chair, a family antique. It looked like another bad month. He had a hard time putting the figures together. It felt like he was missing something, a bill or a note due. Plus he'd have to find the money to replace the missing pieces of equipment and repair the damaged ones.

He looked at Herbert's photo. "Can you give me a clue as to what's going on around here?" Matt said to the black and white image of his ancestor. "I'll take your silence as a no."

Rex was closing up for the night. He walked toward the office to let the boss know about the wet condition of the recent hay delivery. When he saw Matt holding his head in his hands, he figured he'd better not bring it up.

The boss was in one of those moods. The hay issue could wait another day.

"Hey boss, another late one?"

"Yep Rex. Always something. Are we all set for the pack in tomorrow?"

Rex nodded. "I'm switching out Princess for Apache. She has some hoof problems. But other than that we're good."

"I told you about the Kansas gal riding in with us. The one from Kansas? Got a gentle ride for her?"

"Yep, she's on Lady."

Rex held his hat in his hands, nervously twirling it between his rough fingers.

"Anything else you want to tell me?" Matt asked.

Rex knew that, unlike the hay problem, the issue with losing help couldn't wait. "More of the stablehands are thinking about going to that new Legends Stable."

"They are? I figured as much," Matt said in a resigned tone.

"Hal quit unexpectedly yesterday. Left me short handed," Rex said. "Sorry to add to your troubles."

Matt's shoulders sank. He figured this would happen when he learned that competition was coming to town. "If I can't get a handle on all the stuff around here, I might be put out of business."

"Heck boss, you still have the best stables in the

whole area. The locals all love you and your family. Referrals keep coming in right and left. That place is too fancy for me. You're authentic and the tourists love the history here."

"More authentic? That's a kind way to put it. You mean more run down. But thanks for trying. You thinking about leaving too?"

"No sir! I like my job here. You treat me good. And your pappy gave me a hand up when I needed it. A fella doesn't forget that."

"I want to ask you something and I would appreciate an honest answer."

"Yes sir, that you'll get from me."

"Am I as good as my father was at running this business?" Matt's hopeful look caught Rex by surprise.

"Those would be some big shoes to fill. Times were different. One thing I can say is that you treat your family a lot better. Your pappy, God rest his soul now, because he certainly was restless when he was alive, left a lot of the work here to your mother Karen. He was an adventurer who pushed the limits and lost."

Matt cleared his throat and shuffled a few papers on his desk. "So I take it you're saying no?" He looked up at Rex expectantly before saying, "I've been thinking about seeing if the new stables might work out a deal with me to buy this place."

"Now don't even be thinking that!"

Matt laughed awkwardly for a minute before averting his eyes. "I was just kidding."

That didn't sound convincing to Rex. Here he had been trying to defend Matt and the Bender Stables to the other stablehands. And now to hear Matt might sell it out from under them. He couldn't believe it!

Matt continued, "Sorry man, it's late and I'm tired. I'd never do something like that."

"Night boss."

"Night."

Matt closed his computer down and pushed back from his desk. He was surprised it had gotten dark outside. It had been another long day.

15

LILLIA

I woke up excited for the day ahead. Even at this early morning hour the stables were bustling. In one corral, a cowboy trained a horse by keeping her running the outside perimeter of the enclosure. A second fenced area held three horses drinking out of a trough. Two stable-hands sat on the fence watching them, lassos dangling from their hands.

A small group of people, clutching coffee cups, turned when our tires crunched on the gravel drive. Most went back to talking and watching horses being loaded into a long trailer, except for one who waved, calling out to us. Their shout of "Hey there neighbors," carried in unison across the air.

Grauntie walked up to Dorothy and said, "What are you doing here?"

"Our grandson Liam is that handsome young man over there. Liam's part of the outing. Isn't this place so interesting? We've never been here. It's so real feeling."

"I hope so," Edgar said in a deadpan voice. "I wouldn't want Liam to ride into the wilderness on a pretend horse."

"Oh you goof," Dorothy giggled. "You know what I mean."

Edgar leaned down toward me. "Are you a writer young lady?

"No sir, but I'm a horseback rider and these horses look real to me."

He winked at me. "Well that's good, you sound like you're an authority on this outdoor stuff. My grandson should be fine with you along on the trip."

Sammie came running up to me and Grauntie. "Hi! Mom's waiting in the office with some papers for you to sign."

She led us to an old building. "This was the home that my great-great-grandpa built when he moved here. Now Dad uses it for his office," she said with pride.

"Got your warm clothes?" Laura asked. "The evening can be cool because you'll be at a higher elevation. I brought a sleeping bag and hammock for you."

Grauntie said, "Thanks much Laura. Let's sign those papers you need."

"Sorry about the mess in here. Matt's been feeling overwhelmed," Laura said.

Sammie pointed out black and white photographs in dusty frames that hung on the office walls. Grauntie peered carefully at each one. "This is amazing. To have images like this from so long ago."

The man in the grainy photograph moved. I watched as he turned, ever so slightly in my direction. He wore a gun holster on his hips. A lasso hung on the post next to him and a saddle rested on the fence rail he leaned against. I couldn't see his eyes because of the large cowboy hat shading them.

"Some of these are quite rare Nora," Laura said. Her words turned into a low mumble of sounds as I kept waiting.

There he moved again! This time he pushed his hat up…his eyes looked right at me. If I hadn't been staring so intently, I wouldn't have noticed the tiny upward turn in one corner of his mouth. I smiled back.

Grauntie's voice broke in. "Lillia whatever are you staring at?"

"Who was this one?" I pointed at the figure who now stood still and stoic in his cowboy gear.

"Herbert Bender, the founder of these stables. He became quite a legend around here. Not quite up to that of Jacob Waltz, the Dutchman, but in local lore he still holds a place," Laura said.

Well hello Herbert, nice to meet you. I said, "We saw the Lost Dutchman maps at the museum. So that story is true? That he discovered a gold mine that no one else has found again?"

"People believe the gold cache or mine is still out there, waiting to be found. We've had more Dutch hunters come in the last few years than ever before. Lots of them seek my family because of Herbert and his relationship with the Dutchman. Somewhere we have his papers and a few artifacts too. To be honest, I'm not all that into it. Especially because my husband's family sacrificed so much to these mountains. I love this part of the country and wouldn't live anywhere else, but the value to me is the natural beauty."

"Did Herbert have gold maps too? I saw a bunch at the museum."

Laura's smile blossomed. "Now Lillia, are you getting gold fever?"

I laughed. "No I am not, but I know my brother might like to hear about it. He's the treasure hunter in our family."

"He is? That's nice," Laura said, back to searching papers on the desk. "Now where did he leave the release form? Ah, here we are. Lillia, why don't you and Sammie head out and pack up your gear. Nora you have to sign for her as she's under age."

16

THE TRAIL

Orson waited for the group to arrive at the Reavis Ranch trailhead. He watched a small dust cloud rising among the low hills in the distance. Here they come!

The randomness of meeting the writers in the diner and then Nora telling him about this retreat group felt like fate. They will be in awe when they realize I'm going with them. As they should be, he thought.

Orson was extremely disappointed when he heard they'd chosen Bender to pack them in instead of Legends Stable. But being here with the young men, he'd find a chance to promote his affiliation with the new stables. Perhaps he'd make a few uncomfortable moments happen and they'd all agree that Bender Stables had been a bad choice.

He leaned against his champagne pearlescent pickup

truck with Legends classy logo on the side. Glad they'd completed maintenance on it in time for him to make it up here. He glanced in the side mirror to adjust his cowboy hat just so.

The matching single horse trailer lent to the impressive image he wanted to project. Glistening chrome, shiny paint job, styling it right! It was important for him to maintain this prosperous image. He hoped the Bender crew didn't stir up too much dust as he had carefully wiped the wheels clean when he got here. Shame that Bender ran such shabby looking equipment.

Convincing the owners of the Legends to make me the face of their business wasn't easy. It had taken a great deal of schmoozing to assure them that priceless value lay in the legendary figure status I held in this area.

Rumblings that I'm not performing as promised were troubling. That my only value is as a mascot. They aren't living up to their end of the bargain either. They promised me this and that. Well, this and that haven't happened. Now, if they start calling me a phony or a fake legend, I'll give them a piece of my mind. And don't be labeling me a big fish in a small pond!

Orson straightened up, squaring his shoulders. I've got to make things happen or I'll be back to driving my old SUV and riding my sway back mare. If he could only knock the Benders out of business, his position would be safe.

The truck towing the long horse trailer, and a van carrying the writers and their gear pulled into the trail-head parking a lot.

Game on! Here we go!

Rex started unloading the horses. He noted the sweet new pickup truck. No wonder some of the guys decided to change jobs. Fancy stuff like that would tempt anyone.

"Hey Matt. Glad you all made it," Orson said.

"Nice ride Orson! Didn't know you're tied in with that new stable. What are you doing way out here?" Matt said.

"I thought the group might have told you. Being a famous local author, they asked me to mentor them on this retreat. Decided to get myself here as I'm affiliated with a competing enterprise and didn't want to make it awkward for you."

He paused dramatically, squinting his eyes in a questioning manner. "I hope this isn't a problem."

17

LILLIA

Liam asked, "What's he doing here?"

"I don't know. Looks like he's riding in with us. Fancy equipment. I didn't know he owned a stable," one of the other writers said.

"Acted kinda pompous when we met at the diner. Can't believe the dude actually showed up here. Now we'll have to listen to all his bragging about how legendary he is," Liam said.

Sammie tightened cinches on saddles nearby. She called me over. "I agree with those writers. There's something I don't like about that guy. He's been hanging around Grandma lately. Making like he's so interested in how she's doing and everything. Creeps me out."

"Does she think he's hot? Grauntie Nora does," I said.

"Ugh, seriously? I hope Grandma doesn't! She's too

old to even think about that stuff. She just likes to talk to him because he knew Grandpa," Sammie said. "Saddle up Lillia, looks like we're ready to go."

I grabbed Lady's saddle horn, put my foot in the stirrup, and pulled myself up on her back. A good horse, gentle, not excitable. Great to be in a saddle again.

Sammie rode up next to me and reined in Dolly. "I asked Liam if they invited Orson along, and he said it wasn't them. We sure didn't. This is our group, and it seems rude of him to show up with his fancy new trailer and stuff and push his way in on our ride. I bet he just wants to make Dad look bad."

"Ah, come on Sammie. Why would he do that?"

"I don't know, but I don't trust him," she said, before turning to look and make sure everyone was ready to go. "Gotta go help Rex."

Orson moved his horse next to me. He sat tall in his saddle, relaxed hands holding the reins.

"Do you remember me? I believe we met at the Superstition Museum. It's nice to see you again."

I nodded. "You told us about the Lost Dutchman Mine maps."

"Are you a friend of the Benders?"

"Sort of."

Sammie rode up to us, acting all official like. "Excuse

me sir, but we'll be riding out soon. Single file now for everyone's safety."

Orson saluted her. "Whatever you say little lady." He held his horse back to find another spot.

Sammie snarled then muttered, "Little lady? I'm no one's little lady!" She flicked her reins, moving Dolly in place. I fought off a laugh. She sure had something against Orson.

Our group stopped every so often for Matt to point out things, both big and small. When we got to a high point, he showed us the Salt River canyon in the distance and how it formed Apache Lake. Several times he shared the names of flowers we were seeing, from flowering prickly pear and cholla cactus to wild flowers like Mexican poppies and lupines.

The shade from small forests of Sycamore and Palo Verde trees felt cool as we rode through it. We followed the trail past thin, scraggly, dark tangles of shrubs. Occasionally steep slopes of a strange reddish brown color rock rose up beside us, or slipped steeply down away from us. The surefooted horses handled it all with ease.

When we reached another high point, Matt asked us all to dismount. We gathered at the edge of the ridge and gazed down at a lush green valley. Everyone grew silent as if on cue, taking in the scene's beauty below us.

Matt explained that this was the valley that Elisha

Reavis, the Hermit of the Superstition Mountains, escaped to. "It was his paradise. You can see why. Not only are there abundant Ponderosa Pine and Alligator Juniper to shade the hills and valley floor, but at 5000 feet elevation, the air is clean and cool. Most rare of all, the valley holds a spring-fed year-round stream. He had the water he needed for himself and for the vegetables he grew to take to Phoenix and sell. Elisha wisely located his home in this valley and he died near here, a happy man being where he wanted to be, doing what he loved."

The vastness of it all hit me. Here we stood, little in the bigness of this place. Hard to imagine living all alone out here.

"Makes a person feel pretty small doesn't it? Just wait until it gets dark. It's a black darkness like you've never seen," Matt said. "And now, we are entering the lands of the Reavis Ranch…our destination."

18

CAMPFIRE STORIES

The only sounds the group brought were leather saddle creaks, bridle jingles, and hoof thumps on random rocks as their horses followed the trail down into the valley. The Superstition Mountains often inspire this type of silent awe. Man's sense of scale and his place in the world shifts. The string of horses and their riders passed no one.

Death is well known in this vast wilderness. Some disappearances are never solved…the missing simply do not return. The myths and tall tales, the legends and the lies, all come together to keep the superstitious sense of the unknown alive…to keep the legend of the curse alive.

Preparations for camping were quickly and efficiently handled by the Bender team.

Matt had fun showing Lillia and Sammie the knots he used to tie hammocks to trees for them to sleep in.

Getting in and out without tipping proved difficult. A giggling fit ensued every time their sleeping bags ended up a bundled mess on the ground.

Matt said, "You two are quite the pair. But once you get the hang of it, you should be nice and cozy warm. Gets chilly up here at night."

Matt hadn't noticed Orson walk up from behind. "Yep it does. Hope those wanna-be writers packed warm gear too."

Matt cringed. "Wanna-be sounds kind of insulting don't you think? They're my customers. They wanted this experience to get inspiration from the Superstitions. Come on Orson, you love this kind of thing. The mystery of these mountains and the lost gold mines and all that stuff."

"You're right Matt. These mountains are mysterious," Orson said as he turned to walk away." In a slightly sinister tone he added, "Strange things happen here all the time."

Sammie rolled her eyes.

"Don't be disrespectful," Matt scolded.

After camp was set up everyone wanted to do a little exploring. Matt cautioned that darkness drops fast in this valley when the sun is suddenly blocked by the surrounding mountains. "So please be aware of time and angle of the sun. Don't need anybody getting lost the first night. Watch for rattlers, but the scorpions probably won't be out until the day gets cooler. Listen for any animal sounds as mountain lions are often sighted in the area. We'll meet back up here for dinner."

A few hours later, Rex started a fire and began preparations for the evening meal. The campers all found their way back as twilight descended and cooking aromas floated out.

The stars appeared and nature's night sounds joined with the crackling and snapping of the wood burning in the campfire as the group gathered around to enjoy the warmth.

On these trips, Matt likes to tell stories about old Elisha Reavis. This time though he found himself a little intimidated with all the creative writers listening. "Did any of you visit the ruins of the old stone house today? Or the apple orchards? Those were put in after Elisha passed in 1896. He died on the trail between here and town. He was bringing down a load of the produce to sell."

"You might mention that his grave marker can be found not far from here," Orson said.

"Thanks Orson," Matt said. "That's true. Now…"

Orson butted in again. "He died of natural causes, but what with the curse of Superstition Mountain taking so many lives in such mysterious ways, who knows for sure. Right?"

"True. But I'd like to share a different legendary tale now," Matt said. He slowly stood up to his full height. His long shadow leaped out into the trees. Deep pockets etched his face as he spoke. Everyone leaned in closer.

In a soft slow voice he began. "Now I want you all to imagine yourself alone here. Isolated. No one else around for miles and miles. Except for Apaches...who move silently...stealthily...unseen. Apaches who don't want people like you living here."

When the fire popped, shooting bright embers out, Lillia and Sammie jumped.

Matt's voice lowered, drawing attention back in to his story. "And imagine you are a strange looking white man with long, tangled hair and a thin, scraggly beard. You've made your home here, but it is threatened by the Apache warriors. You can feel them. They've been watching you."

Everyone's eyes were glued on Matt. "Then you see them! Indians in full war paint ride in, circling your home. Trouble has come to your quiet valley."

Matt looked each person in the eye, one by one. "What would you do? Is there hope? Pray? Hide? Run? They're upon you...it's now or never!

Matt had everyone holding their breath as he said, "Elisha knew what to do."

Then in rapid succession Matt said, "He stripped off all his clothing, got buck naked, and came running at the approaching warriors like this…"

Everyone gasped, leaning back wide-eyed as Matt let out blood-curdling yells and began a twirling wild dance around the fire ring. Stomping and hooting. Until out of breath, he sank back down to his log seat.

The campers erupted in laughter and everyone started talking. *Why did he do that? What happened? Crazy old man. Did the Indians leave alone?*

"But Dad," Sammie asked. "Why didn't they kill him?"

"Elisha knew that the Apache believed that loco crazy people possessed supernatural powers and that the Great Spirit protected them."

Liam asked, "But couldn't they see the old guy was alone. They could just kill him anyway."

"True, but Apaches believed something else. And that was the key. They believed that a person inherits the soul of whatever they kill."

"Smart guy that Elisha. He knew they wouldn't want to carry around a crazy white man's soul with them."

"That's right!" Matt said.

19

LILLIA

A campfire always meant comfort and coziness to me. People gathered together. The night chill held back. Sparks lifting off into the darkness. Darkness pushed away. So why didn't it now? Was the aloneness here so overpowering? Was it knowing how isolated we were? Creepy shadows were thrown into the surrounding darkness. Tossed up against a tree one moment, then dancing against a different one the next. Was I seeing some of those Apache warriors hiding in the darkness?

Maybe I was just tired after a very long day. I watched Orson fix his eyes on me, a snide smile came to his lips. "See a ghost Lillia?"

Then he stood and let out a big yawn. "Time to hit the sack for this old cowboy. Hope you all have great dreams that inspire good written words."

The others excused themselves too, thanking Rex for dinner and Matt for his stories.

Sammie and I fought to get into our hammocks. I tumbled out twice before Matt came over and held it steady for me. The giggling lifted my mood.

Without firelight affecting my vision the valley floor around us looked magical. The full moon brightened up the dark landscape, creating soft blue moon shadows.

"Mom told me she's going to take some photographs from Kitty's patio tonight. She calls this a Super Moon cause it's so close to the earth or something like that," Sammie said.

"Your mom is cool. I love her pictures. Grauntie likes to take photos to put in her digital frame. She says memories bring smiles."

"I like that idea. Mom's photographs are mostly of landscapes, or cactus. Pretty stuff, but usually without people in them."

"I'm picturing your mom and Grauntie on the patio looking up at the same moon we are."

"Do you miss your mom when you're gone on these trips?" Sammie said, "I bet she misses you. You've got a brother too?"

I didn't know how to answer Sammie's question about missing Mom. But I told her, "And a little baby sister too. I had another little sister once, but she died before birth."

"Oh no! That's so sad. I bet it just broke your parents' hearts. Wish I had a brother or a sister."

Sammie was sincere in what she said. But remembering those times only made me upset all over again. "Yeah, guess so."

"Lillia, why so weird about it. Sounds like there's more to what you're saying. Tell me."

Simply hearing those two words made my own words flow. I told Sammie about Chloe, my brother Charlie's twin, who didn't live.

"So they knew she would not be born alive?"

"Sort of. The four-year-old me told them there was a baby and a dolly in Mommy's tummy. But they didn't believe me. I was so little. What did I know?"

Sammie's mood shifted. "Guess I'm not getting what you mean. How did you know?"

"I have what Grauntie calls a special ability. My imaginings. I was just an innocent kid. But when the birth happened, and my so-called dolly was a stillborn baby, Mom totally freaked out. She rejected me. She feared me."

"I'm sorry to hear that. But it was years ago. Did she get over it?"

"Sometimes I think so. I always hope so. I keep trying to prove to her that my special abilities can be used for good. That I understand them better now. So things are okay for a while. But then something snaps and I feel her looking at me and remembering all over again."

"I get it. Adults can be weirdos sometimes. What I don't get is how you imagine stuff like that. Is it like being a psychic?"

"No. Least I don't think so. I mean I'm still trying to figure it out."

"Let me know if you have any imaginings around here. Cause maybe you could help my family."

"With what? Do you mean the troubles at the stables?"

"Yeah. Odd things happening there. Each one is no big deal I guess. But just the quantity as Dad says. He's starting to think it's the curse again."

"The curse of the Superstition Mountains?"

"Right. My grandfather and great-grandfather mysteriously died in the mountains so I can see why he might think that."

"Whoa! Really? That's scary."

"I know. I think he feels he's failing us too. Especially Grandma, because she gave him the stables to run. I've seen him looking up at our ancestors' portraits and asking them for help. Not saying he's crazy, but, ah you know what I mean." I heard the hopeful tone in her voice.

I asked, "What I just told you about me...do you think I'm crazy?"

"No way Lillia! I'd like to have a specialness like yours. I'd like to be invisible and I could sneak around and see who's messing with the family."

I felt relief because I'd been called crazy and laughed at too often in the past. And it hurt.

"Maybe's Dad's making too much of things…trying to honor our family's legend? My great-great-grandfather Herbert Bender was kinda famous around here I heard. But so much of that legend stuff is hooey. I mean come on. Was there really a Dutchman Mine that no one else has ever found? How do you lose a mine? All the stuff they say to fake it for the tourists. Like those people pretending to get hung in Goldfield. I mean, who does that? Or that posing in old western clothes with guns and stuff."

I said, "Hey we almost did that! It looked like fun. What's wrong with having a little pretend fun?"

"Sorry, but I see it differently." Sammie reached over, her hammock bumping into mine. "But I didn't mean to make you feel bad."

"I say it's innocent fun. People pay big money to watch actors dress up and talk on a stage. Tourists come here wanting to feel they're living part of the past."

Sammie and I talked awhile longer as we lay looking up at the night sky.

I didn't tell many people about my ability and I liked it that way. But it felt good to tell Sammie.

20

A SUPER MOON

The same moon that shone down on Reavis Ranch deep in the Superstition Wilderness, appeared in the lense of Laura's camera as she focused for another shot. She wanted to capture the super moon at this special time when it was close to the earth. She was in the moment, ready to shoot when someone walked across the scene.

Darn…who would be out at the edge of the desert this late?

"Hiddy ho," Dorothy called as she and Edgar shone their flashlight toward the patio.

Nora rose from the chaise lounge she had been sitting on. "Well hello there neighbors!"

As they stepped over a low decorative stone wall, Dorothy tripped.

"Oops my dear," Edgar said as he steadied her.

Dorothy giggled. "Couple of old goats like us got wandering off into the desert to see the full moon. Time got away on us."

Edgar noticed Laura. "Sorry, we didn't see you there. Why don't you turn some lights on?"

"Edgar honey, no lights because she's taking a photograph of that outstanding moon," Dorothy said. "Sorry, hope we didn't ruin your shot."

Laura smiled and said, "No problem. I've gotten all the shots I want."

"We love love love your work Laura," Dorothy said. "And because of you, I am assured our friends are glad to see us at least once a year!"

Edgar popped his eyebrows up, paused, and said, "Because we bring them your photo calendars!"

"Oh you two are too cute!" Nora said, "How about we turn on some lights and I bring out the wine and snacks? I insist you stay, you've had a long desert hike and need some nourishment."

Dorothy did a dramatic swipe across her brow. "Ah yes, it has been an exhausting few minutes."

"Sounds perfect," Laura answered.

Edgar said, "I'll give you a hand."

"Dorothy, you've got quite the gentleman there."

"Yes, he's a keeper. I meant to ask you about that handsome man we've noticed with Karen. Might I ask if they're a couple?"

"I don't know of anyone she's seeing. My father-in-law passed away more than a year ago so I suppose it's possible. What does he look like?"

"Very handsome older man. Dresses really sharp. And wears his mustache ooh-lala," Dorothy said, fake fanning herself to emphasize her words.

"Does he wear impractical cowboy type clothes? Like boots that are too shiny? Or clothes too pressed?" Laura asked.

"Why yes! That's a perfect description."

"That's just Orson." Laura dismissively waved away any importance. "He's always trying to get Karen to tell him about our ancestor Herbert Bender because he knew the Dutchman and Reavis. Orson writes what I consider not very good books about the legends around here. Tries to paint himself as the authority on all things Superstition Mountain related."

Dorothy persisted. "Looked like more than that to me."

Nora returned carrying a plate of cheese and crackers with small bunches of grapes at the edge. Edgar carried four wine glasses holding the stems between fingers of one hand, and an open bottle of red wine in his other. "Now Dot dear, you're not spreading gossip are you?" He sat a glass down in front of her and poured her wine, before pouring another and taking it to Laura.

"Thank you Edgar. I think it disappoints Dorothy that Orson's not wooing Karen," Laura said with a wink.

Nora said, "Lillia and I met him at the museum. He seemed very nice. Talked to us about the legends of the area."

"Personally I think he's a legend in his own mind," Laura said.

"Ouch, that's rather harsh don't you think?" Edgar said.

"Not really. He's full of himself. Suppose you might have to do that to sell books about the Lost Dutchman Mine. They are a dime a dozen. My husband's family probably has more personal knowledge about all that than anyone. But people don't want reality, they want to cling to their dreams. I suspect Orson plays on those people for his own benefit," Laura concluded.

"Now dear, don't be too hard on those dreamers. Sometimes it's just a fun passion like a hobby," Dorothy said.

"Sorry," Laura said. "Sometimes I can get carried away."

Nora raised her glass saying, "Cheers to a beautiful moonlit night in Arizona with friends."

"Here, here," Edgar said.

"And here's to our intrepid adventurers up in those mountains looking at the same moon as us," Dorothy said. "Now pass the cheese, please!"

21

LILLIA

I woke in the night and couldn't get back to sleep. I slipped out of my hammock, hoping I'd be able climb up in by myself later. Soft snorts and shuffling hooves from the horses nearby was comforting. Between the trees, I saw their deep blue, almost black shapes. All else eerily quiet and still.

Wonder what it felt like to be Elisha and his burro when they lived here all alone? Did he find comfort in having another breathing living animal friend with him?

I made my way to a big rock near the campfire and blew at the ashes to see if the fire would relight. Nothing. I pulled my legs up against my chest and wrapped my arms around them.

A haunting sound came from the hills. An owl or the wind howling? The last dying echo of a shout?

Under the cold black heap of the campfire a glow appeared. Small bright embers flickered up through the ashes. Guess there's still a little life in there. I leaned over and gently blew on it again. A flame sprang to life. When I sat back up, I wasn't alone.

Three other figures had joined me around the campfire...and they weren't the other campers. I watched as their images steadied...solidified. They didn't notice me. I sat still, allowing my imagining to take form.

"Quite something isn't it? Seems like the biggest moon I ever seen."

Another man poking at the fire with a stick spoke. "Surprised to see you two up this way. Been prospecting?" He looked up, flames reflected in his eyes.

"I know how you hate visitors Elisha but we figured it was about time to check in on you. Got yourself a nice place here old man." The person talking reached over for a small tin coffee pot. "Why do you like this isolation? Doesn't it drive you just a little crazy?"

The man with the beard must be Elisha Reavis! I'm sitting right where he used to live. I'm picking up the pieces of his energy. Wait until I tell Sammie!

"Herbert, to me this is paradise. I have water, food, and my freedom."

I smiled inside, but kept still. That's Herbert Bender!

"And I'm not alone now am I?" Elisha chuckled.

"Even when you two leave, I got me all sorts of companionship out here. There's my sweet little burro, loyalist friend and helper a man could ask for. I got me this fine valley whispering me to sleep at night. I ain't alone."

"Nothing like a fine woman waiting at home with a hot stew or children to hug goodnight," Herbert said.

"I got me a good burro too, but I'd miss meeting friends to share a whiskey and a game of cards," the third man said.

"It's my way. Been among too many people in my life. This suits me just fine. Jacob, you're one to talk. You been back in these hills all alone many a time. Is that gold cache of yours running out any day soon?"

Jacob Waltz! The Dutchman, that's who the third man was. I wish Sammie could see this.

Jacob took the coffee pot from Herbert and poured some into a cup sitting on the ground between his legs. "Nope it ain't. But my strength is running out on me. Thinkin' I might just settle down in town. Wish I had done things a little different. Maybe stayed with that woman I left behind in Kansas. Or had me a child who'd take care of me. Gold is cold comfort in old age."

Herbert said, "The missus keeps getting on me 'bout staying around closer to home more too. Dang I hate to admit it, but these mountains keep tempting me."

"See what I mean," Elisha said. "I've got it simple

here. Only one I answer to is Gertie there." He cackled and slapped his knee. "And she don't complain. Might be you are trying to have both women…the missus and the mountains."

Jacob almost choked on the coffee he was sipping as he laughed, sipping into the fire. It sizzled. "Good one Elisha!"

"Hey now, don't go putting out my fire. I worked hard to get this going."

Herbert raised his coffee cup to his lips and took a long sip before speaking. "You might be on to something there. She's always saying how she hates these mountains. It's like I'm fighting another woman for your attention she says.…one I can't compete against."

Murmurs of the three men's talk continued, even as their figures faded away. Then all was quiet, leaving me alone again.

Why had my imagining powers shown me Elisha Reavis, Jacob Waltz, and Herbert Bender enjoying each other's company on a quiet night deep in the Superstition Mountains? I may never know, but it was fun.

I managed to snuggle into the hammock without falling. Next thing I knew, morning sounds and smells woke me.

22

MORNING MYSTERY

The morning sun rose behind the tall mountain, but the light hadn't yet reached down into the Reavis Ranch. A morning campfire was lit. Odors of fresh coffee and frying bacon wafted out.

Matt gave Sammie's hammock a push to wake her. "Time to get up!"

"Morning Dad," Sammie moaned, turning away from him and pulling the edge of the sleeping bag over her head.

"Grab some breakfast before it's gone. We'll be taking off in about half an hour."

Lillia poked her nose out, then her arms stretching them straight up. "I'm awake too." She moved and ended up rolling out of the hammock! "Ouch!"

Sammie muffled a laugh. "Smooth moves."

Rex was almost done feeding the group when Orson walked up asking for more bacon and eggs. "Sorry but I have to save some for the girls. We didn't plan on having another person here."

"Humph...would have thought you'd always throw in a little extra," Orson complained.

"Here you go," Liam said. "You can have the rest of mine. I'm not so hungry."

"Why thank you young man," Orson said. "I didn't realize my being here would make things like breakfast so complicated."

Rex ignored the remarks as he cleaned up after breakfast. "Hey Matt, who do these coffee cups belong to? I don't remember them being part of our gear."

Matt said, "Their not ours."

When Rex asked if anyone else had brought them, answers of *not mine, don't know, nope*, came back. Hmm...odd. They look authentic he thought. This here is blue enamel. The real stuff.

Rex set the cups aside and started discussing the wet hay issue with Matt. "We need to move it back outside into the sun to dry more as soon as possible. It's getting too overheated."

"I wish you would have mentioned it. Stuff like that can self combust," Matt said. "It'll have to wait until tomorrow though. There's too much else to do this afternoon."

Orson stood to one side polishing off the eggs on his plate and listening to their conversation, an idea forming in his head.

23

LILLIA

I couldn't believe my eyes! Pieces of my imagining had stayed behind. Those three cups were still by the fire pit where I'd seen them last night when Elisha, Herbert, and the Dutchman drank coffee out of them. But I said nothing.

Orson picked up the cups. His eyes pinched in concentration. He asked Matt, "What do you make of these? We are the most experienced men here. Look like authentic antiques to me."

"Yep, typical of the type of cookware that would have been used here years ago. We often find old stuff like that up in these hills."

Sammie said, "But Dad, they weren't here last night. And no one says they found them anywhere and put them there."

"Can I please keep them as a souvenir? I mean if they are not all that valuable to anyone," I said meekly.

Orson's look hit me like a spotlight. "You? Why would you want some old miner's coffee cups?"

I gulped. Now what should I say? "Ah my Grauntie likes old stuff. I could keep one for a memory. And ah…"

"Fine by me," Matt interrupted. "I'm sure the museum has plenty. All I know is we need to get going. Hand them over to her."

I reached for the cups dangling from Orson's hands. Orson pulled his hand back and held on to the cups, still staring at me. "I guess that's good by me too." Then in painfully slow motion he extended them toward me.

Our hands accidentally touched as I took the cups from him. He trembled ever so slightly. Just for a fleeting moment his eyes opened wide and the cups almost dropped out of our hands.

Sammie was calling. "Lillia, come on. We've got to get you back to the stable. Remember you're going to drive the Apache Trail today. Hurry up."

I turned and ran to my horse without looking back at Orson. I left the campsite at Reavis Ranch with the three cups strapped securely to my saddle.

24

THE ARGUMENT

Later that day, after Matt, Rex, and the girls had left, the writers were each quietly working on their own manuscripts. Orson however, strolled about looking at everyone's work, much to their annoyance.

Liam had just written...

These mountains have secrets. They know what happened to those intruders long gone. The ones who never returned home. The ones whose bones are uncovered years later.

These mountains hide the truth from the lookers. They know what they seek is buried beneath the surface. They know the lure of the hunt.

These mountains are a temptress to those willing to heed her siren's song.

"Almost poetic, but that use of personification is

rather overdone," Orson said as he peeked over the Liam's shoulder to read what he had written.

Liam gritted his teeth. He hadn't asked for Orson's opinion. "Thanks man, but I'm just experimenting with my thoughts. Not meant to be read by anyone else."

"Certainly. Excuse my intrusion. Just thought you might appreciate an informed opinion," Orson said. Because you sure could use it, along with more skill he thought. Trite words, almost a plagiarism. You jokers wanting to be writers. I have yet to witness it in any of you.

Orson couldn't help but remember the strange jolt and the flash of an image he'd had when he touched Lillia's hand while exchanging the cups. Last night he'd overheard snippets of conversation between the two girls. Lillia said she could imagine things. What the heck was that supposed to mean? That girl spelled trouble. So did that Bender brat complaining about all the troubles. Poor Bender Stables. Blah, blah, blah. He'd had to choke back a laugh when Sammie talked about her family being cursed. If only she knew.

Now Karen Bender was different. She was easy to manipulate. Commiserate with her and she was putty in his hands. She expected her stupid son to run the stables like her husband had. She would never admit to the fact she was the one who really ran the business when her husband was alive. Too bad about the mountains' curse getting him, just like it got his old man. Wouldn't be long until she agreed with kind, caring Orson and accepted the buyout deal he'd negotiated with Legends.

But just in case, knowing he couldn't stall much longer, he moved his plan up.

It had to be done tonight.

His instincts had been right before.

He needed to act.

* * *

Back at Bender Stables Karen yelled, "How does a business function with such a mess?" With a swift sweep of her arm she sent all the papers on Matt's desk flying.

Bones took a quick step back, moving as far away from her as the small room allowed. *I shouldn't have called her with my question. Now Matt will be in some big trouble when he gets in.*

"I asked you a question." Karen spun and glared at Bones, her face sharpened with anger. "Who are you anyway?"

"Bones ma'm. They call me Bones. I'm new here so's I...ah I don't know...," Bones stuttered.

"Oh for god's sake, who left you in charge?"

Matt had just gotten back and walked in as Karen

pushed the old wooden desk chair, sending it spinning into the wall. "Whoa, what's going on here?"

Bones breathed a sigh of relief. "Hey boss, you were gone and I couldn't find the papers for the next trail ride…"

"So who does he call? Not you, not Laura, but me. I didn't expect to be handling all this when you agreed to take on the business. I figured I was done with it." Karen's voice rose with each word spoken.

Matt calmly said, "It's okay Bones, you can leave. Please help Rex get our horses unloaded."

Bones wasted no time in sliding out the door, almost running into Rex. "Slow down man. You almost took me out. Matt, do you know where today's bookings are? Guess the guys can't find the list of horses we need to take to…"

"I do not know Rex," Matt said, his voice unnaturally enunciating every word, trying to get control of what was happening here. "Saddle up ten horses in case we have a full group. Please take extra release forms with you in case you need them."

"Will do. Morning ma'm, I didn't see you there," Rex said.

Karen stood glaring at Matt. Without looking at Rex she snipped, "Morning."

Rex backed away from the open door, giving Matt a *what's up with her* look.

Matt watched his mother take a couple of deep breaths, trying to get herself under control. But he realized she wasn't succeeding when she blurted out, "I should have taken the offer. But no! I had to let you try your hand at this. Now look at the mess we are in."

Karen caught herself up short. She never meant to say that. What was happening?

"I'm sorry, but what did you just say?" Matt's jaw clenched. He needed to be careful with his words. "What offer?"

Laura walked in and gave Matt a big hug. "Welcome home honey. I came to pick up the girls. Oh here they are now."

Sammie and Lillia came running in. "Hi Mom! Grandma, I'm glad you're here. We had the best time! Thank you for setting the trip up." She hugged Karen but slowly backed away when Karen didn't return her gesture. The awkwardness was obvious.

Laura quickly ushered her and Lillia back outside. But she heard Matt say, in a very alarming and angry voice, "Mother, answer me."

25

LILLIA

Sammie's mom hurried me out of the office before I even had a chance to say thank you to Karen.

"Sorry Lillia, but something more must have gone wrong with the business. They're having another little argument," Sammie said, embarrassment written all over her face.

"It's okay. See you tomorrow?"

Grauntie's car pulled into the drive.

"You're only here for a couple more days so we'll be sure to get you two together again. Enjoy the Apache Trail drive today!" Laura almost pushed me up to the car to hurry me out of here.

"Hi," Grauntie said, as she opened her car door. "Did you have a ..."

"You two better hurry along. It's a long drive and

there will be lots of places you'll want to stop and explore," Laura said. "Be sure to visit the cliff dwellings near Roosevelt Dam. Bye now!"

"Ah okay. Please tell Matt thank you again," Grauntie said, a confused expression on her face.

Sammie waved goodbye.

As soon as we left, I told Grauntie about the situation in the office and how uncomfortable it made me.

Grauntie said, "I agree. There's more happening than we are privy to. Family businesses are often complicated. I'm sure they'll be fine. Now, tell me about the trip."

I told her about the horseback ride to Reavis Ranch, the beautiful sights along the way, the sleeping hammocks Mr. Bender set up for us, and the stories around the campfire.

Grauntie listened to everything and asked lots of questions as she maneuvered our car along the narrow gravel road snaking through the mountains. She worked hard to avoid the rough spots and areas that had washed out with the recent rains.

"And you'll never guess who showed up. That man you got all gaga over at the museum. He has the most gorgeous Palomino horse."

"Ha-ha! I'm hardly the type to get gaga as you say. He's an author so he'll probably help the group with their writing. What were those things you put in the back seat?"

I glanced sideways at Grauntie. Her hands lightly gripped the steering wheel and loose tendrils of her gray hair danced in the wind. Dust from the roadbed rose behind us and drifted away across the rugged landscape. But I didn't answer her. I wasn't ready to let her know about the imagining.

Her wry smile appeared. "No answer? Hmm…let me see, what's that line you always use? I'll tell you about it later?"

I had to laugh. I often used that line with her. And I always did end up telling her later.

"You don't have to say a word now. But you better tell me all about those cups on our flight home. Deal?"

"Deal! How do you always seem to know stuff like this? You must have some specialness like Grandpa had," I said.

"No, I don't think so. But I pay attention to my intuitions. And more importantly, I know my great-niece pretty well by now!"

26

FAMILY TROUBLE

Laura didn't know what to do anymore. Matt was so stressed and Karen wasn't herself these days. But when she saw what was happening at the office in front of staff, she knew that they needed a family conversation. Karen ran the business with an iron hand until she lost her husband. That loss took so much out of her. It hadn't taken much convincing to let Matt run the day-to-day operations.

Laura tried to stay out of Matt's family business. Her focus was on her own photography business which was growing. She didn't want to get in the middle of helping with Bender Stables, but it appears someone needed to step in. She thought Matt was doing okay, but maybe things weren't going so well, at least not to my mother-in-law's standards. Laura felt the anger rising up in her. Matt was doing his best. Get off his back.

Laura sent Sammie to help get the horses ready for the trail ride at Goldfield. Then she headed back to the office to help Matt face his mother.

Back at the office Karen and Matt were still locked in an argument.

"I asked you what offer was made that you wished you had accepted?"

Karen dismissively waved him away. "Never mind. It doesn't matter now."

"And why did you make such a big deal about the trail ride papers in front of Bones?" Matt said, no longer controlling his tone. "He looked scared out of his mind."

"This place is such a mess. No wonder you lose things. You have no sense of order. Laura should help you with the bookkeeping. Instead she plays around with her ART! I was always here when your father was alive."

"Yes and look how that went. You grew to hate working with the stables. And Dad was always gone. Do you know why? He couldn't wait to get away from here. Away from you."

"How dare you! This place would have fallen apart if I hadn't taken on a strong role."

Matt breathed deeply. He might say something he'd live to regret.

But Karen pounced on his silence. "No answer? I

want a full accounting by tomorrow morning. I've trusted you without supervision for too long."

Matt looked over his mother's head and toward the door. He gasped, "Honey?"

Karen spun and saw Laura standing in the doorway. How long had she been standing there? Snatching up her sunglasses and purse, Karen pushed past Laura. "Excuse me dear, I have some things to take care of."

27

LILLIA

We'd just driven past the Roosevelt Dam when the sign for the cliff dwellings at the Tonto National Monument appeared. Inside the visitor center we watched a movie. It was an overview of the history of this area and how the ruins were preserved. I learned that people who settled here and built their homes in the caves high in the surrounding cliffs, used the Salt River or Rio Salado for irrigation to grow their crops. Archaeologists named the culture Salado because of that. When they moved away in the 1400s, no one knows for certain where they traveled to.

I stood and looked up the trail that would take us to the cliff dwellings. I was in awe. Farming down by the river meant they had to walk up this path constantly. It was a super steep climb.

Grauntie stopped to rest and catch her breath on one of the benches. I didn't mind, it was hot out here and I was breathing hard too. The slopes surrounding us were covered in cactus, flowers, and small shrubs. Signs posted on the edge of the path identified each type. We were about halfway there. How did they do this everyday?

A park ranger greeted us at the entrance to the dwelling. The ranger explained the Salado were a peaceful agrarian society, agricultural based. She pointed out the various rooms in the cave and what they had been used for. "You can see actual handprints on the walls. And come along this way." She took us into another small space. "That black film on the surface is smoke residue from their cooking and heating fires."

From the heights, and through the cave's broad opening, I saw Roosevelt Lake sprawling across the valley below. Government employees had dammed the Salt River many years ago to form Roosevelt Lake and to provide a water supply for Phoenix. The river that had irrigated this sprawling valley hundreds of years ago still flowed somewhere in that lake. Its waters passed through the dam and on to form the Apache Lake that Matt had pointed out to us yesterday.

The ranger's voice faded away.

A warm flush rushed over me.

I smelled wood smoke rising from the stone fire ring

next to me. The paved path we'd just walked changed to a narrow pebbly foot path that ended at a ladder leaning against the opening of this cave. I watched as a young girl and boy climbed the ladder up from the path to the dwelling's floor where I stood.

A woman squatted on a stool next to me, turning from the baby she was tending and looking toward the children with joyful eyes. They pulled woven basket-looking backpacks filled with corn from their shoulders and set them near the fire. More walls and rooms formed around us. I heard other people talking and laughing in a language I didn't understand. A colorfully decorated pottery jar holding water was being hauled up by a sturdy rope from the path below. Soon the smiling face of a strong young man with black hair appeared over the edge of the entrance. He leaned his body against the ladder and called out to the children to help pull the jar in.

The baby cried. The woman, her brown skin crinkled by age and sun, gathered him up and rocked him, crooning in a soft sing song voice. When she suddenly hugged the baby tighter, I realized she saw me. She covered him with a blanket, as though protecting him from the unknown danger I presented. I can't imagine what my shorts and t-shirt from hundreds of years in the future looked like, but I tried to appear as unthreatening as a strange twelve-year-old kid from the future could.

No one else seemed to sense me as they moved about...preparing dinner...weaving a new basket... cutting up a strange prickly looking leaf...playing a game.

I hugged myself and rocked too, just like she had been rocking the little baby. I gestured with open hands if I might see him. She nodded. I slowly walked the four steps to her and squatted down next to the low woven seat she rested on. She pulled the soft covering away, and I saw him. He rested peacefully in her arms. I kissed my fingertips and touched them on his chubby cheek. And just like that they all disappeared.

Grauntie and the ranger were still talking. I closed my eyes and breathed in the cool earthy smell of the dwelling, trying to hold the image of the baby boy. I raised my fingers to my cheek.

"Lillia, for heaven's sake why are you standing there with your eyes closed. You're right at the edge. Open them up so you don't fall."

I kept them closed a second longer while whispering goodbye to the boy from hundreds of years ago.

After thanking the ranger we headed back down the hill. At the bottom I turned to look back. High up in the shadowed entrance to the cliff dwelling the old woman appeared again, the baby still cradled in her arms. Hard to picture what this all will look like moving centuries forward. But for now, I know I'll always have the warmth of that baby's plump little cheek with me.

Soon we were on our way back to Apache Junction and a nice evening swim.

After driving for miles, I saw the sign for the Reavis Ranch trailhead. "Grauntie, look, there's the sign for the trail we took. Want to see where we started our ride?"

"If it doesn't take too long, we should keep moving so we get home. I'm not good with driving long once it's dark out," Grauntie Nora said as she turned down the narrow drive.

When we got to the empty parking lot, I opened my car door and pointed across the scene before us. "Isn't this cool? Come here Grauntie, look you can see the Salt River far away in the distance." I grabbed her by the hand and led her to the best viewing spot."

"These views are amazing! I'm so happy you had fun on this trip Lillia," she said, wrapping one arm around me. "But mostly I'm glad you still want to travel with this old lady."

We stood a moment longer to take in the sunset view over the nearby peaks and the softening mountain shapes fading away in the distance.

28

SLIPPING AWAY

Just hours earlier, Orson had left the very parking lot where Lillia and Nora stood enjoying the view across the Superstition Wilderness. What he set in motion would send shock waves across the community of Apache Junction.

One building, Orson had thought. Just one of the old crumbling buildings. The one with the hay stored in it. Yes, that one should do it. The hot hay self-igniting would be blamed. He wished it didn't have to come to this, but he had to seize the moment.

His self-righteousness quickly squelched any small sense of guilt that tried to rise up in his gut. *They are forcing me do this. How is a man supposed to do all the Legends Stable owner is asking of me?*

Let Bender's collect the insurance money and we'll all win.

Orson's sudden announcement to the group that he would leave to spend the rest of the day away was a welcome surprise to them. He'd have been shocked to know this, but as usual he was oblivious to what others really thought of him.

"Have a lead on the goldmine location?" Liam teased him.

"I wish," Orson said in good humor as he swung himself up into Blondie's saddle. "Don't wait dinner on me. I won't be back until after dark. I will enjoy traveling by the light of the moon. Enjoy your day all!"

Now that he had a new plan he was excited to get on with it. Orson had ridden Blondie out of camp, loaded her up in the trailer, and left the Reavis Ranch Trailhead. He drove to an abandoned home out in the desert near the Bender Stables and unloaded her again. He would need to take a short horseback ride to his final destination.

All the small nicks at making trouble had started weeks ago…loosening a bridle, throwing a rock to startle the horse…tedious conversations with Karen hinting at how poorly Matt was running the place…had done their job.

He was sure this last act would seal it. Soon Legends

Stables would swoop in and take Bender's business away and he'd be sure to be front and center, making certain his position as a legend was intact.

He rode Blondie toward the stables assuming he was unseen. After he'd completed his last small nick, he slipped away, back to the trailer where Blondie was once again loaded in. Out of the goodness of his heart, he placed a call to report the possibility of a fire at Bender's.

He drove away whistling a happy tune, the night air blowing in through the open windows. When the first sirens sounded in the distance, he let out a loud laugh. A haunting sound that echoed, bouncing off the cliffs and the valleys, the mountains and the plateaus.

The deed is done.

Now back to camp and my waiting sleeping bag.

29

LILLIA

We'd been driving in darkness for over an hour. The night air was cooler, but we kept the top down and turned on the car's heater.

We were leaving the wilderness now. Short strings of glittering lights, like diamonds on a necklace, lined up in the darkness where houses sat along the desert roads. Back to civilization.

Then I started catching glimpses of an unusual yellow light toward Apache Junction. "Are you seeing that light ahead?" I asked Grauntie.

"I am. Might be one of those hot-air balloon glows."

"What is a balloon glow?"

"You've seen the hot-air balloons around here right? They use a fire to heat the air in the balloon and that makes it rise. Sometimes at night, they keep the balloons tethered down, but the propane fires are lit so the inside of the big balloon looks like it's lit up. Want to drive that way and try to find it?"

"Nah, that's okay. I'm ready for the pool."

But as we drove closer I began to smell smoke. Something else was going on. "Grauntie, something's on fire and it's not the inside of a balloon."

Without warning sirens screamed behind us. Grauntie pulled to the shoulder of the road. A fire engine flew by followed closely by another one. An ambulance raced by us next.

We pulled in behind them. As we turned the bend in the road, we saw the fire up ahead. Flames leaped up into the night sky.

The fire was burning just outside Apache Junction in the hills above Goldfield Ghost Town.

30

LONG AGO

150 YEARS AGO...

Three figures huddled around the campfire at Elisha's ranch in the Superstitions as a soft, velvety twilight settled in the lonely valley. Sliced potatoes and onions sizzled in a cast iron pan suspended over the fire. The skin of the roasting chicken hanging from a spit was browning to an appetizing crisp.

Herbert pulled the saddle from his horse's back and, with a grunt, dropped it on a boulder. "Gettin' too old for these long days in the saddle."

Elisha cradled one of his blue-speckled enamel coffee mugs between his hands. "I'm feeling a few more aches myself."

Julia Thomas brushed the dust off her clothes. With a sigh of resignation, she hugged her horse's neck before joining Elisha and Herbert by the fire.

Elisha watched her slow approach and waited until she settled on a log seat before saying, "I'm so sorry for your loss Julia. You were a good friend to Jacob. We all know how you nursed him at the end. He was lucky to have you."

"It was your loss too. I know how much you enjoyed each other's company over the years." Julia replied. "Got a cup of coffee for a tired old gal?"

Elisha grabbed the coffee pot's hot handle with an old rag to pour a cup for Julia. "Careful now, it's plenty warm," he said. "Sorry you and Herbert didn't find the old Dutchman's cache of gold or his mine or whatever the heck he had up in them there mountains. Was hopin' the map he left would point you right to it."

Herbert exchanged amused grins with Julia. "So did we. Been trying to decide if the map is real or not."

"I have to think it is," Julia said. "I asked nothin' of him, especially not the box of gold he left under his bed for me nor this map. He was my friend just because he was. Not like with some who saw him with those gold nuggets and they suddenly were his best buddy. He was a lot like you two," Julia said. The flames image danced in her eyes as she looked from Herbert to Elisha. "Jacob was okay with people up to a point. After awhile he had to get back to the mountains. Until he got sick and hunkered down in that little shack on the river. Worst spot to be when the flood came. Got himself the breathing sickness, and that took him."

Elisha said, "Well I hope when my time comes death takes me quick. Not dragged out sick like he was. Hope I die quickly and quietly on a mountain trail. Alone before God. Not in a bed laying there waiting to catch my next breath."

Herbert stared at the campfire lost in his thoughts until Elisha asked him, "What about you?"

Herbert looked up at his two friends. "Reckon I picture dying with my family around me. Much as I love my time away to wander in these hills, I want them holding my hand when the good Lord takes me. Guess when it comes down to it and a man faces death, he don't get himself a choice." Herbert straightened up. "Enough of this talk. Let's have us some of those taters and chicken."

Elisha carved the chicken with his hunting knife and spooned potatoes on to all three plates. When they'd had their fill, the conversation turned back to Jacob Waltz.

"I remember that night Jacob died, and you came to me with the box he had under his bed," Herbert said. "You were one sad and confused gal."

Julia laughed. "I still am. He left me gold which I'm mighty grateful for. But that darn map. I felt the gold fever first time I held it." Julia opened the leather pouch lying at her feet and pulled out a folded paper. "But the fever's gone. I've decided I'll spend some of the gold fixing up my bakery real nice with a new oven and cupboards for supplies. I'm done with chasing around looking for the gold."

"Folks in town will get wind that Dutch left you his treasure," Elisha chuckled. "Some of them old menfolk will come sniffin' around."

Julia's laugh echoed across the dark hills as she shook the paper open in the night air. "Let them. I'm going to make me some copies of this here map to sell. Send those gold hunters on their way with it. Just cause we didn't figure out where Dutch's gold was doesn't mean someone else can't. Right Herbert?"

"You got that right Julia."

"I'll call it the Lost Dutchman Gold Mine map," Elisha said. "Watch my word, he'll be a legend one day."

"Good idea," Herbert said. "Gold hunters will gladly come buy your map. And who knows, but they might find the mine like you said. I'm thankful Jacob convinced me to build a business and take care of my family. He used to say what waited for me down at my home and my stables was priceless."

The three friends told more Jacob Waltz stories well into the night.

Many a Lost Dutchman Mine story would be told

around campfires in these Superstition Mountains over the years to come and the legend of the Lost Dutchman Mine would grow.

Now...

The campers at the Reavis Ranch in the Superstition Wilderness spent the evening preparing dinner and then enjoying the simple meal in the cool mountain air.

They discussed the writings they'd worked on during the day. Critiquing one another's work was part of the discussion. When Liam's turn came he said, "I came here excited to be part of a writers' group and on a retreat. I brought my work in progress, looking forward to polishing it. Giving my characters more depth. Taking the plot lines to completion. But instead I've been, oh I don't know what to call it, but perhaps distracted is the right word."

One of the others called out, "Trying to make an excuse for good old writer's block?"

Everyone laughed at first, but something stilled them when the sounds were eerily swallowed up by the emptiness. They looked uneasily at the moonlit landscape around them, then leaned in closer to the fire's flames.

Liam continued, "We all just felt what I've been trying to capture in words. This place has a presence of its own. A life force. I've experienced nothing like it. I know this sounds cliche but I get goosebumps here."

No one spoke for several minutes. Nature's night sounds amplified. Unseen figures wove among the trees. The hills breathed.

31

LILLIA

They cordoned the area off with police cars blocking the road before Grauntie and I got to see what was burning and making that black sooty cloud above the Bender Stables. We jumped out of our car and ran along the edge of the road toward the fire.

I searched the small crowd of people watching the firemen working to put out the blaze. Where are Sammie and Mr. Bender? I was just with them this morning. Someone was being loaded into an ambulance. The paramedic slammed the back doors shut. He jumped into the driver's seat and turned on his lights and sirens. Everyone moved to clear a path for him to leave.

"Did you see who it was?" I asked the surrounding people. No one seemed to know. I watched it speed away toward the lights of Apache Junction far in the distance.

This was a scene from a horror movie. The flashing rotating lights bounced off the smoke wall that rose up before around us. The intense stench of moist hay burning cut through the air. Silhouettes of horses being led away from the fire, rearing up, fighting against the person trying to save them. And most horrible, above all else, the frightened whinnies cutting sharply through the chaos.

"Please everyone, step back. We need to clear this area in case any of the other buildings catch on fire," a uniformed officer said. We all shuffled further to one side but soon began to creep closer toward the flames again.

"There's Sammie," Grauntie shouted, pointing to a small group of ghostly outlines standing in the smoky haze across the property. "Come on Lillia."

The officer stopped us again. "I can't let you go further. You'll only be in the way."

A figure came running toward us. It was Karen. She looked so distraught. "Officer, please let us through. I'm the owner of this property and these are my friends. I need to get to my granddaughter."

"Yes, of course Mrs. Bender. I'm sorry I didn't recognize you. Please be careful though," the officer said. Another ambulance was making its way up the long entrance road toward us as Karen led Grauntie and I to where Sammie stood.

We ran to hug each other.

I was so happy to see she was safe.

32

NIGHT OF THE FIRE

"My god, what happened?" Karen asked Sammie. "Where are your mom and dad?"

Sammie sniffled and wiped her eyes as she pointed toward the burning building. "They are in there somewhere trying to save the horses. I want to help but they made me wait here!"

"Do you know how this started?"

"When Mom and I got here, she said it might have been the wet hay bales. Then she said I had to stay right here before she ran into the fire."

Grauntie said, "We used to have barn fires in Kansas that started like that. If the hay hasn't dried properly, a reaction begins and often ends with these horrible results."

"There she is! There's Mom!" Sammie shouted, excited to see Laura.

Lillia asked, "Why is the horse she's leading out blindfolded?"

Karen kept her eyes on the scene as she said, "Horses try to run back into their stalls where they have always felt safe…even if it means returning to a stall on fire. They can be controlled better when blindfolded. Oh good, look Sammie, there's your dad, he's got Dolly! Your horse is getting out safely."

Grauntie stood with her arm around Lillia's shoulder and Karen hugged her granddaughter close as they watched the barn Herbert Bender built generations ago, burn to the ground. And just as they said prayers that the fire would be contained to one building, it jumped to the nearby equipment shed.

Far away in the dark Superstition Wilderness, Orson quietly returned to the remote site at the Reavis Ranch. He and Blondie had managed to stay on the trail by the light of the moon.

Calling in to the fire department as he pulled away from the Bender Stables might have been a mistake. He knew they tracked phone calls by the cell towers. He'd be sure to delete it from his phone later.

Don't be paranoid he scolded himself. No one will ever suspect you. Anyway, that hay was wet and on the edge of self-igniting.

Comfortable with his decision and the action he took, he settled himself in his sleeping bag for a good night's rest.

It was well into the early morning hours before the fire was extinguished.

Laura and Matt watched the area being marked with yellow crime tape. They'd sent Sammie home with Karen earlier.

Saddles and gear were piled haphazardly around the grounds, waiting to be assessed for damage. Friends and neighbors had promised to return in the morning to help with cleanup.

All the horses had been saved. Some were corralled a safe distance away. A few escaped into the hills. The crew from Legends Stables promised they'd search and find the loose horses in the morning.

33

LILLIA

Grauntie was still sleeping when I slipped out of the house in the first light of dawn. Warnings about walking alone on the hill behind the house and heading up toward the mountain rattled in my head.

Be sure to have water.

Watch out for rattlesnakes.

Don't lose sight of the house.

But I ignored them because I needed to move around and would only go a short distance. Over that ridge ahead and then I'd turn around.

When I reached the top of it I had a great view of the stone Indian maiden pinnacles on top of Superstition Mountain. Below me I saw a wash. It looked like an easier walk back, not so many cactus or rough scrubby brush. I scrambled down the low bank and into the dry riverbed. It was amazing to think water ever ran through here. Now it held only a soft sandy soil extending as far as I could see.

After I'd been walking I thought I'd better climb out of here and make sure I'm heading the right way, back toward Kitty's house. The walls of the wash were much higher and steeper now. The banks of reddish-brown rock with sharp needled bushes were hard to climb. My feet slipped, and I ended up using my hands to lean against the slope and scramble out.

When I reached the top, I couldn't see any houses.

Even at this early hour the heat was rising from the desert floor and I had no water with me. The harsh wall of Superstition thrusting up was the only landmark I recognized.

I was lost.

Walking towards me was the man from the museum with his burro. "Morning Lillia. Out for a stroll?"

Had I told him my name? Grauntie must have. I guess I looked confused because he said, "Sorry if I startled you."

"It's okay. I was just surprised to see anyone else. I've been taking the wash back then it felt like the walls were closing in on me so I climbed out and there you were. Does water ever run through it anymore?"

"It sure does. Flash floods happen quite often here,

especially during our monsoon season." He pointed up toward the pinnacles on top of the mountain. "Have you heard the legend about those gals? They saw one of the biggest floods ever."

"I read the story on a sign at the museum. But that's just a myth isn't it? I mean those rocks weren't really Indian maidens."

He laughed and shrugged. "Ain't my place to say. The story was told by more than one tribe. It was handed down through generations."

I had to laugh too. "And they didn't have cell phones to document the flood with a photo like everyone would do now right?"

"Cell phones?"

"Mobile phones. You know? With cameras right in them."

"Cameras in phones? Like telephones that Alexander Bell invented. I read something about that."

"Ah, now you're teasing me," I said.

A puzzled look crossed his face. "I wasn't teasing you. I really didn't know."

"Oops, sorry," I said.

"Legends, myths, tall tales...they all start with some truth. Settlers heard other stories from the Indians too. Strange sounds in the hills. People disappearing. Mysterious deaths. The Indians held a fear of these mountains. They said it was cursed. The white men figured they were just superstitious Indians, so that's what they named this mountain."

"So that's how it got the name," I said. "I thought it had something to do with the Lost Dutchman and all the gold hunters who can't find his mine."

The man chuckled and mumbled softly, almost like he forgot I was there. "They're just looking in the wrong place."

I looked at him more closely. He wasn't the reenactment guy from the museum. His clothes were different, more worn out. The burro was carrying different things, odd tools, leather bundles.

With hesitation I said, "I saw Jacob's maps in the museum."

"You don't say?" He considered what to say next. "Don't get too swept up in it all Lillia. We humans sometimes create legends out of thin facts."

"So you think the maps aren't real? That he didn't find gold."

"No, didn't say that. Just that stories tend to grow when there's gold involved. Greed can make a man do some crazy stuff. It's part of the danger, the curse. "

I was unsure what more to say to this stranger. "Well, guess I should get back. I'm a little turned around here though." I didn't really want him to know I was lost…too many stranger danger lectures.

"When I'm gone, you'll see the way to go. We were glad you took the cups we left for you."

Goose bumps broke out! "Are you Jacob Waltz?"

He gave a big smile behind his bushy beard. "Glad you finally recognized me. Guess you didn't remember me from the night at old Elisha's place. We knew you were watching us by the campfire."

"You did? But you didn't talk to me then."

"Lillia, you know how you feel you can't control your imaginings?"

I nodded.

"It's random from our end too. We couldn't talk to you back then. But at least the cups made it across," he said. "And now I'd best let you go. Just popped in to tell you to use those cups to reach us if you need anything. Oh and when I'm gone you'll see the way to go."

As he walked away from me, I saw Kitty's house on the horizon beyond him.

34

MORNING NEWS

Nora read the local paper's report of the fire as she sipped her morning coffee on the patio.

The Bender family suspects the source of the devastating fire was improperly harvested and stored hay that-self combusted. However, this reporter received a scoop that the state fire investigator would be on scene today. Though insurance carriers routinely investigate for arson, it is highly suspect that the state would get involved in a situation like this.

Luckily an anonymous caller phoned in a report of flames at the Bender Stables and within ten minutes of that call the fire engines were on site. However, because of the age of the building, the flames had already burned through the roof. Lack of a sprinkler system and low water supplies hampered fire fighters efforts

All horses were successfully evacuated or escaped. One person sustained serious burns and smoke inhalation and is in critical condition at the local hospital. His name is being withheld pending notification of family

Goodness this sounded terrible, Nora thought. She looked up to see Dorothy and Edgar walking in the desert.

"Good morning neighbor!" Edgar called out.

"Come join me for coffee," Nora said. "Have you heard about the fire at Bender Stables?"

"Goodness, no!" Dorothy gasped. "What on earth happened?"

Nora's finger held her place in the article. "Lillia and I saw it last night when we returned from our drive. Just reading this morning's paper to see what more has been discovered."

"Please read aloud. Oh dear this is just awful," Dorothy said. She leaned forward eagerly as Nora read to them…

When questioned about the possibility of arson, owner of the stables Karen Bender is quoted as saying she cannot imagine who or why anyone would do such a thing. She is certain it will prove to be just a horrible accident.

"Arson?" Edgar vigorously shook his head. "I can't believe it either. That family is so well loved around here. They're legends in this area. Old Herbert Bender started that business decades ago. No one would wish them harm."

"Arson? That's phony baloney," Dorothy said.

Karen and Sammie joined everyone on the back patio. "What's phony baloney?"

Dorothy ran up to hug Karen. "I'm so sorry about the fire. Is everyone all right?"

Edgar piped up, "Including those beautiful horses?"

Karen took a seat at the table next to Nora. "Yes, except for one of our stablehands. He's still hospitalized with smoke inhalation and third-degree burns. I'm heading over to the hospital as soon as they allow visitors in. Is that today's paper?"

Nora pushed the newspaper toward Karen. "It is. Your quote from last night is right here. We all agree with you. No one would have done this on purpose. I'm sure they'll discover it was the wet hay."

"Where's Lillia?" Sammie asked.

"She's still sleeping," Nora replied.

"No dear," Dorothy said, "She's out for a walk. We saw her far away, up on the big ridge toward the mountain."

"Dorothy gave her a big shout, and I tried my loudest longest whistle," Edgar said. "But I don't believe she saw us."

Nora looked surprised. "She left so early by herself? Not good."

"Want me to go look for her?" Sammie asked.

Nora stood on her tiptoes, her eyes searching across the desert. Her anxiousness faded when she saw Lillia's small figure in the distance.

35

LILLIA

I saw the Dutchman again! I haven't told Sammie about the campground imagining yet. I'll tell her after the fire stuff settles down today.

People on the patio waved to me.

Grauntie scolded me as soon as I came in range of her voice. "Lillia Pameroy, never leave like that without letting me know. Did you have any water with you? You could have gotten hurt out there."

Dorothy fervently nodded her head. "Why Edgar and I got turned around just last week. We got behind these scrawny looking trees and then just drifted along on the easiest path and before you know it we were up behind Legends Stables."

"So technically we weren't lost Dot," Edgar said as he tapped one finger on his chin.

Sammie started to giggle, and I soon followed.

Dorothy chided Edgar. "Well we could have been if we hadn't seen their buildings."

"Hmm, I guess. But we saw them Dot…and so…we weren't lost."

Dorothy let out a huge sigh. "Please Edgar, I'm trying to impress Lillia with what could have happened to her out in the big open desert." She turned to me, "You understand what I mean right?"

"I do and thank you. I should have left a note. Sorry Grauntie."

"Why did you take off like that?"

"After the fire last night I was shook up. I'd seen nothing like that and I guess I just needed to clear my head. How is everything going there?"

Karen said, "I'm on my way over to help with things."

Sammie quickly added, "And I hoped you would want to come along Lillia. It would mean a lot to me."

"You go with them Lillia. I'll stop in town and pick up some coffees and sandwiches," Grauntie said.

"That would be sweet of you Nora," Karen said. "Thank you. We'll see you there."

36

SHERIFF BARNEY

Sheriff Barney Fitz had always been in awe of the Bender family because of their legendary reputation in this area. He had compassion for them because everyone said the curse of the Superstitions had taken two family members. This morning would be an uncomfortable situation because it appeared that someone had deliberately set the fire. According to everyone, Matt Bender was the last person at the scene. Had the curse struck the family again?

A car accident or domestic dispute brought out nosy neighbors. But fires were the worst. He'd spent most of last evening just getting people to clear the way for fire trucks and the ambulances. He didn't get involved in any investigative work. In fact, he felt like the fire department had kept him out of the circle. He'd change that this morning.

He was ready to assess the situation in the light of day. How much damage had been done? What would the fire investigator determine? He understood that they had treated Matt Bender for burns and his hired hand, Bones, was still in an induced coma because of his injuries.

Barney puzzled over why anyone would believe Matt wanted to burn down the barn. It just didn't seem right to him.

There were numerous vehicles already at Bender's. Besides official fire department vehicles, there were pickups, horse trailers, and semi trucks delivering more hay. He reached for his sheriff's hat on the passenger seat and set it squarely on his head. He used the rearview mirror to check that his badge was on straight. Next he put his aviator style, dark lensed sunglasses on. He got out of his police cruiser, hitching up his gun belt.

Matt greeted him. "Morning Sheriff."

"Mornin' Matt. How are the burns doing?"

"They'll heal." Matt held up his bandaged left arm. "I'm worried about Bones. This afternoon they will start bringing him out of the coma. I want to be there. Excuse me, but my insurance company's representative has questions for me."

Barney started to walk along with Matt. "Matt, I

didn't get to tell you last night how sorry I am that this happened to you and your family."

"Thanks Sheriff. And I appreciate you helping keep things under control last night."

A pompous looking woman in a dark suit, her hair pulled sharply back from her stern face waited near the shell of the second building. When she saw the sheriff approaching with Matt she said, "If you'll excuse us Sheriff, I'd like to talk with my client alone."

Barney pulled up his figure to its full five feet eight inches before saying, "Yes ma'am, I have other important work to handle." He waved his arm in a vague direction and kept his back stiff as he walked away in case she was still watching. He decided he'd head over to talk to Rex who was working with a group cleaning saddles.

Laura came up from behind and grabbed Barney's arm. She seemed upset and rightfully so after what she has been through.

"Sheriff Fitz, you know Matt wouldn't have done this! Look at that insurance adjuster. She's practically accusing him of it. Why are they even suspecting that? It's got to be the hay combusting. The insurance company is just trying to get out of paying the claim for damages."

"Calm down Mrs. Bender. Matt didn't do this. It'll all get straightened out," Barney said. He shifted uncomfortably. He didn't like to see women crying. "There, there now." He patted her arm. "Oh look! There's your mother-in-law with that cute girl of yours."

He practically pushed her toward Karen's car. Lord, what was he going to do to prove Matt innocent? He'd never handled a case like this. And what if that young stablehand didn't make it?

This could turn far worse!

37

LILLIA

When we pulled in the Bender Stable's parking lot I was amazed at the buzz of activity. A pickup with a small horse trailer attached pulled in beside us.

The woman driver leaned out. "Morning Karen, we rounded up one of your mares over toward the museum. Where should I take her?"

Karen looked around in confusion. "I'm not sure what to tell you Josie. Matt's over there. Check with him. Oh, and thanks for your help neighbor."

"That's what neighbors do." Josie said. As her trailer pulled past us, the big brown eyes of the horse she'd rescued peered out from one of the small windows.

Laura came up. It looked like she'd been crying. "Karen, park up over there. You'll be out of the way. They want to bring in some equipment today to take down what's left of the ruined buildings and stabilize any of the damaged ones."

When we parked, Sammie leaped out to hug her mom. "There are so many people here helping! Don't be sad. It'll be all right."

I felt bad for them. It would take a long time to be back to normal.

Rex came walking up to Karen and Laura. He spoke in an exasperated tone. "Can I make some decisions? Everyone wants to help, but Matt has been tied up all morning with the inspectors and insurance people."

"Of course Rex. Please help take charge. I trust you," Karen said.

Rex nodded, compassion returning to his voice. "Appreciate that ma'am. Think you two had best head over there." He tilted his head toward where Matt stood, his shoulders slumped, as the woman talked, gesturing and pointing with her long bony fingers. "Matt's in a load of hurt."

38

TROUBLE STIRRING

It relieved Matt to see his mother and wife headed his way. He had to get away from this annoying woman. Couldn't she see all of her concerns had to wait? He had people counting on him. And he had to get over to check on Bones, but what had he been doing here so late last night? Why was he caught up in the flames?

"Mom," he yelled. "Can you come here?" He introduced Karen to the insurance woman and said, "My mother owns the stables so she can help you better than me with some of these details."

The woman sniffed. "These aren't mere details Mr. Bender. But you…" She turned toward Karen and curtly nodded, "…and your mother, need to understand that all the repair and business going on now will not be covered in an insurance claim should the outcome of the fire investigation prove to be arson. I just want to be totally clear on that point. Good day." She spun and strode away, weaving between the piles of burned lumber, the horses being led to the corral, and the people milling about.

Matt's eyes pleaded. "Mom, you know I didn't do this."

Karen said nothing.

Laura said, "We know honey."

"Is Sammie with you Mom?" Matt asked Karen.

"She brought Lillia along and they went to find Dolly."

"I'm glad." Matt hadn't talked to Sammie since late last night. What was his little girl making of all this? He had to figure out how to clear his name.

Karen sighed and looked at the destruction around her. "So much history gone. I remember we used to carve things in the boards of that old barn. Your dad showed me where other Benders had marked the walls with horse names, or jotted down a new foal's date of birth. Your dad and I kept up the tradition. We were so excited to preserve that area." Her words caught in her throat.

Sheriff Fitz cased the scene. He listened to conversations and even conducted some interviews, being sure to make notes of words and impressions in the small spiral notebook he kept. Apparently some unusual things had been happening. Damaged gear. Broken halters. Spooked animals. Mismanaged paperwork.

And then there was Bones. He was a new hire. Sounded like a young drifter. He would have to question him. No doubt about that. How did he get caught in such a bad situation? Why was he there so soon after the fire started? Could he know something about it? Or did he see what happened?

People who lived nearby mentioned seeing office lights on late into the night. That Matt seemed to never catch up with paperwork. It appeared he was losing stablehands to the new operation across town. Seemed everyone had information to share. Course he would have to evaluate the worth of it and weed out the lies and exaggerations.

That reminded him of a conversation he had one day with Orson. He had let slip something about what a poor financial position Bender was in. Even questions whether his insurance was up to date and stuff like that.

Gosh, he hoped that wasn't it. Finances have pushed more than one person to do something stupid. Stop it! It can't be arson. That family has suffered too much.

He shook his fist at the mountain. Don't you dare turn your curse on this family again!

39

LILLIA

The woman walking away from Mr. Bender was cartoonish…all sharp edges.

"She looks mean. Like Cruella de Vil in a suit." I said.

"Glad she finally left. I'm worried. If they think Dad did something like start a fire for insurance money, they're crazy!"

"Wish there was something I could do to help."

Sammie's brow furrowed, and she pinched her lips. "There has to be. What about those special abilities you talked about? Could you figure out what happened here? It's sure looking like someone set it on purpose."

"And counted on not being caught cause everyone would think it was the wet hay starting the fire," I said in agreement.

"Right. So what do you think? Can you pull up an imagining like you said?"

"I've been trying. But I'm not picking up anything."

Sammie looked crushed. "Come on Lillia, let's take Dolly off to a quiet spot away from all this. This parking lot is like Grand Central Station. Someone pulls out and someone pulls in. Hope things get back to normal soon."

I had a sudden flash. Of another parking lot. The one at Reavis Trailhead. It was empty yesterday. Why? Orson's truck and trailer should have been there. But it wasn't!

"Sammie, I have an idea. And maybe even a suspect."

"What? You know who did this?"

"Maybe I said. There are some puzzle pieces that might help us figure it out. I remembered something from yesterday that I now realize is very odd."

Sammie grabbed me by the shoulders and shook me excitedly. "Out with it! Tell me who. Tell me what you remembered."

I didn't want to go around accusing someone of something so awful until I could get more proof. But how? Understanding that my friend Sammie's father might go to jail for the arson left me no choice but to try. "Is there a policeman investigating? Someone we can trust?"

"I suppose the sheriff. Though he seems kind of bumbling to me."

"Is he here now?" I asked. "

Sammie took a quick look around. "I don't see him right now. Come on Lillia, just tell me! Is it Orson?"

With my sharp intake of breath, Sammie knew her guess was right. "That guy is no good. What clue have you got?"

I explained about the empty parking lot where Orson's horse trailer should have been. "But don't get too excited Sammie. Maybe he just left early."

"Or maybe he snuck out to light my family's stables on fire!" Sammie was practically screaming at the end of her sentence.

40

ORSON POUNCES

When the campers at Reavis Ranch learned about the fire via the radio phone, they were shocked and confused, wondering how they would get picked up and packed out of here.

Orson took charge of the situation, telling them he would ride Blondie out to the trailhead, return to town, and make sure that arrangements for the groups pick up were made. "I'll see to it that the Bender Stables issues don't stand in the way of your safety and well-being."

Liam stood to one side trying to figure out why he just had such a hard time warming up to the guy. Sure he was full of himself, but lots of writers and artist types were. But this felt different. Oh well, what did it matter anyway?

As Orson began the trip back to Apache Junction he

felt elated…almost jubilant. Things were going his way. This was really happening. Surely Karen would see that the Bender Stables were becoming a thing of the past. Locals would say the Superstition curse had hit her family once again. He would encourage that thought. Then a light bulb went off. *I'll write a book about the Benders and title it Cursed by the Superstitions!*

When Orson arrived at the stables, he looked across the scene trying to grasp just how much damage the fire had caused. Sammie and Lillia were on the top of the hill with her horse. Matt was working with Rex and Laura directing helpers. Karen stood off to one side near the office. When she entered the small building, he quickly decided to join her.

"Karen, I'm so sorry to hear about this." Orson said as he snuck in the door behind her.

She jumped. "Orson, you scared me."

"I came as soon as I learned about the awful fire. I had to be here to support you in whatever way I can. Have they found a cause for the fire?"

Karen's eyes teared up. "The inspectors are certain it's arson."

Orson's eyes widened as he stepped back. "No! Who on earth would do something like this to such nice people?"

"They are waiting to question one of the stablehands

who was seriously injured in the fire. He was here right when it started and tried fighting it by himself. The authorities said that often the arsonist wants or tries to be the hero too." Karen touched Orson's arm and steadied herself. "But," she paused and took a deep breath. "I just find this so hard to say…"

Orson held his breath. Surely there was no way they suspected him.

"They suspect Matt." She broke down and choked back a sob. "How much more can this family take?"

Orson put his arms around her even as a snaky smile pulled at the corners of his lips. "You've suffered too much already Karen. They can't really believe it's him."

Karen didn't know what to believe. She pulled away from Orson to look at the portraits of the Bender men. Her husband and his father…disappeared in the mountains…their bodies never recovered. At least Herbert's death had come uneventfully, peacefully, surrounded by his family…no curse on him.

She turned to back to Orson. Her voice was weak, without conviction. "It can't be Matt. I refuse to believe that."

This was the moment. "Karen, some things are just out of your control. The curse of the Superstitions has struck again. Whether it was the stablehand, or god-forbid your son, either way, you'll get no insurance coverage."

He paused, letting her realize that what he said was true. "I think I can still get the owners of the Legends to make you a good offer for the place."

Karen said, "Even with the fire damage?"

A sudden rattling sound startled them both. "Sounds like they are really going to work," Karen said with a deep sigh. "I hope they can save the other damaged buildings."

What neither Karen nor Orson noticed when they left the office, was that the framed photo of Herbert Bender now hung at an odd angle.

41

LILLIA

Sammie and I found the local sheriff leaning on a paddock railing. He was looking very serious as he paged through a small notebook.

When Sammie told him what I had seen yesterday, he just said, "Thank you for bringing me your concerns but we can't just pull things out of the air and make an accusation like you're doing. Orson might have decided to leave camp early. We've got a full-fledged fire investigation going on. You leave the serious business to us big guys. Okay?"

"But it's my dad who everyone is accusing. And he didn't do it!" Sammie stomped her foot in frustration. "You've got to consider all the clues."

"It's not looking good for your father I'll give you

that, but I am going to interview another suspect soon as I get the okay from the hospital."

It silenced us both. Another guy? Who could that be? Were we wrong?

"But Sheriff, will you check up on Orson too? Can't you call on the radio phone to the campsite and see if he's there?'

"Someone looking for me?"

We all spun at the sound of Orson's voice.

The sheriff cleared his throat and said, "Hey there Orson. We were just discussing you."

My heart was beating so hard I was sure they could all hear it. I looked over at Sammie and she didn't seem nervous at all. She was glaring at Orson. "Where were you last night?" she asked him.

"Why I was at camp. You know that Samantha. I rode out on my own for part of the day, but stayed in the general area of Reavis Ranch. Why?" Orson's wicked I gotcha grin stopped Sammie in her tracks.

The sheriff pointed at me. "This little gal says she saw your trailer was gone from the trailhead yesterday. How do you explain that?"

"That she's confused." He paused to let his next words sink in. "Or she's lying."

Sammie started to say something, but I nudged her and she got the hint.

"Sheriff Fitz, don't be too hard on these two. Give them a little slack after all that has happened. You would be upset too. We all want the truth about what happened."

"Yes sir, we do. Sorry to bother you Orson."

"No problem. We received a radio phone call at camp this morning, and I left to help out here."

"Why that's mighty nice of you," Barney said.

"I'm only doing what any good neighbor would." Orson patted me and Sammie on our heads as he walked away.

This time I pinched Sammie. She must not react!

The sheriff's phone rang. He listened. "Thanks for letting me know. I'll be right over." He hung up and said, "You run along now girls. I've got to go interview our other suspect."

42

THE TIN CUPS

Sheriff Barney Fitz turned on his siren as he left the Bender Stable. He'd received a call that Bones was being brought back to consciousness for a short window of time. The hope was that he would be able to breathe on his own.

After listening to the girls, he was concerned that the investigators were settling too soon on the obvious suspect, Matt. Starting a fire for the insurance money was, sad to say, not an unusual thing to have happen. But all his senses told him that Matt didn't do it. He was on a mission to reveal the real culprit.

The police car, with flashing lights on and sirens blaring, left the stables just as Nora pulled in. What on earth happened? She entered the bustling parking lot. Goodness but things were moving fast here.

A pickup and long horse trailer pulled past her, heading over to a big corral at the rear. Hopefully that meant more of the missing horses had been rounded up.

As she bumped across the ruts to find a place to park, the three tin cups Lillia had brought along yesterday clinked and clanked. I must be sure to pack them in our luggage before we leave for the airport tomorrow she thought.

43

LILLIA

Sammie was mad! "That's what neighbors do," she said with a snarky tone. "Those words coming from his mouth make me CRAZY!"

I couldn't help laughing, and Sammie heard me even though I turned my back and covered my mouth.

She gave me a little shove. "Not funny!"

She couldn't fool me with her hands on her hips looking angry. She was starting to fight back a grin too. "Some ace detectives we are. So now what Miss Pameroy? Where's that imagining power you said you had? Hmm? Could sure use some right about now."

Grauntie walked by carrying a large covered box. "Girls, could you please go back to the car and bring the other containers up here? These are sandwiches and drinks for the people helping cleanup."

Sammie and I raced to the red convertible to get the food. I gasped when I saw what lay on the floor of the back seat. The three cups! The ones my imagined Jacob Waltz had just talked about this morning!

Sammie was reaching across the seat for a bag of plates and napkins as we locked eyes. "What?" she whined.

"I know where I can get some imagining help." I grabbed up the three coffee cups.

"Are those the old tin cups Rex found by the campfire?"

"Yes they are and I'll tell you more, but first let's take this food stuff to Grauntie," I said.

44

SUSPECTS

After talking with Bones it didn't take long for Sheriff Barney Fitz to know that Bones hadn't done it. Nonsense about an arsonist trying to be a hero and then staying to save the destruction caused by a fire he had just started. Bones was just a young kid who fell on some bad luck. He had earlier learned that Rex let him stay at the stables, unbeknownst to Matt, until his first paycheck came in and he could get a place of his own.

The boy was in horrible pain and would soon be sedated again, but he wanted to tell the sheriff everything he knew. He told how whiffs of smoke woke him, but by then flames were licking at the second-floor hay loft where he lay. He struggled to breathe as he stumbled to find the trap door with its ladder that would get him downstairs and outside to fresh air. But the flames were too hot. He clawed his way to the big opening of the upper loft door to get a breath of air.

Bones was struggling to say more.

"What is it? Did you see something?" Barney said.

Bones coughed harshly again. It was getting too hard to breathe. A nurse rushed in and told the sheriff he'd have to come back later.

Sheriff Barney Fitz knew he was considered a bit of a bumbling fool by many, but he always trusted his instincts...and now they told him the kid didn't do it. And Matt Bender didn't do it either.

Where those two girls on to something? But how to prove the possibility of a third suspect. He had to handle this carefully. His first action would be to go back to the Bender Stables and try to find more clues.

45

LILLIA

After we dropped the things off at the food tables Grauntie was setting up, Sammie quickly pulled me back to the issue of the fire. "Okay, now tell me what's up. And does it mean we can prove Orson started the fire?"

"I think maybe we can. First, I want to tell you what happened during the night when we were camping." I looked around for a spot where we could talk without being overheard when I noticed the nerdy looking boy, my spirit guide. In a goofy jerky motion he bobbed his head toward the office door. Office it was.

The place was empty. I shut the door and gave Sammie a quick overview of me seeing the three men around the campfire drinking out of these cups. Before she could say anything, I quickly added that I'd seen Jacob again this morning.

Her skeptical look surprised me. "So when you came back to all of us waiting on the patio, you're telling me you'd just talked to Jacob Waltz, the Dutchman? Give me a break Lillia. How do you expect me to believe that?"

"I know I shouldn't have told you!"

"Wait. No. Sorry. Seeing ghosts I get somehow. I guess. I mean it seems possible. Oh I don't know what I'm saying." Sammie looked torn and confused. "Seeing things, imagining them like you call it is one thing. But telling me you talked to a ghost, and that he said, like okay call me up on an old tin cup?" Sammie picked up one of the cups and held it to her ear, mocking me.

I grabbed it away from her. "Sammie stop. I need you to help me. I have an idea."

"An idea from a ghost?"

"From this cup, and with help from that guy up there." I pointed to her great-great-grandfather's photograph on the wall.

"How is he tied up with this?"

"He was one of the men at the campfire."

I held the cups close against me and closed my eyes.

46

AGAINST THE LAW

Matt took a break, grabbing a sandwich and a soda. It felt like the longest day and it was only late morning.

He was defeated. He didn't start the fire. But who did? There's Bones. Might he have started it accidentally? When Rex confided in him that Bones had been living in the stables he had reacted with anger.

"We can't allow that."

Rex hung his head, and did that twirling his hat in his hands like he always did when he was nervous. "I know, but every time I tried to talk to you, there always was another fire you were putting out."

Matt gritted his teeth. "That's an awful way to put it."

"Sorry boss. Bad choice of words. The kid just needed a boost up. And now I feel awful that he's in such critical condition because of what I did."

"What do you mean what you did? You didn't start the fire. But Rex, give me an honest answer."

"I always do."

"Do you think Bones might have done it by accident?"

"No way! I spoke to him when they were taking him into the ambulance. He could barely speak, he was in so much pain. But he swore on his mother's grave he didn't cause it."

"Then who did it Rex? I'm at my wits end. Who would do such an awful thing?"

Orson watched as they unloaded more captured Bender horses from a Legends trailer. He couldn't wait to close the deal with Karen for the purchase of the stables. He watched Karen, Nora, and Laura serving sandwiches and coffee to the people helping with cleanup. All goody, goody and nice while everyone slaved away trying to help.

Hammering sounds echoed across the hills as carpenters attached boards and braces to stabilize the buildings that were damaged. Whiffs of leather cleaner came from the group removing soot from saddles and bridles. His lungs felt the acrid sting of smoke that hung over this place. Even so, Orson was breathing easier now. It seemed certain they'd confirm it was an arson fire and there was no way they could prove it was him.

He felt uneasy about that kid in serious condition. If he dies, there will be a second-degree murder charge out there. But that wasn't his fault. How would he have known someone lived in the stables? That was against the law. The kid shouldn't have been there.

47

LILLIA

The photograph on the wall rattled. I opened my eyes and there stood a tall muscular man with the deep brown tan of an Arizona cowboy. Herbert Bender! Hooray!

I took a calming breath before saying, "Thank you for showing up. I need some help."

Sammie punched me in the arm. "Of course I'll help you. We talked about that. But what can we do?"

She couldn't see him! He grinned and took the cup from me.

Sammie's eyes popped wide open. "Please tell me I'm not seeing that cup floating across the room!"

"You're not. Well sort of. Touch it."

"No way."

"Come on Sammie. It's okay."

She looked at me then back at the cup a couple of

times before she gingerly reached out and touched it, immediately pulling her hand away.

"I mean grab it," I said. "And don't let go!"

When she took the cup by the handle, I could see by her wide-eyed, mouth open expression she saw him now too.

In a trembling voice she said, "Lillia, is this who I think it is? Or am I seeing a ghost?"

"Like I said, you can call him a ghost but I like to say he's my imagining. Whatever you prefer. Samantha Bender, meet Herbert Bender."

Herbert's eyes softened as he looked at Sammie. "I understand you're turning into quite the horse wrangler. I'm proud of you."

The cup was shaking because Sammie's hand couldn't stop trembling.

"It's okay. He's here to help," I said. "This cup is the connection to him."

Sammie still didn't speak, but she clung to the handle of the old tin cup, her eyes locked on Herbert.

He looked toward me. "I don't want to scare her. Should I leave?"

There was a loud gasp right before Sammie shouted. "No!" She looked startled as the word flew out of her mouth. But then laughed with tears running down her cheeks. "No one will believe this!"

Whew! She was okay. I would have to talk to her about what she told anyone later, but right now I needed information.

In a matter of minutes, Herbert Bender answered my questions and confirmed who started the fire at the Bender Stables…Orson.

Sammie continued clutching the tin cup, and I let her. We were in this together.

Herbert ended by saying, "Jacob always regretted telling anyone about the gold he'd found. It drew too much attention to him. Attention brought its own circus of characters and stories and problems. My friend must have decided to reach out to you this morning and let you know how to reach me because my family is getting the wrong kind of attention now."

Sammie said, "I knew it! Mom calls Orson a legend in his own mind."

Herbert laughed out loud. "Now that's a perfect description for this character. He's been working hard at becoming a legend by damaging my family's business and reputation to achieve it. Go get him girls!"

Herbert faded back into the photograph.

Sammie let go of the tin cup and with a clear sharp clink it hit the floor between us.

"Let's get this done," Sammie said, with furrowed

brow and clenched jar. She pumped her fist in the air toward Herbert's portrait. "For the Bender family!"

"So he confirmed it was Orson to us, but how do we prove it to the sheriff?"

"We'll make him listen. We have to."

Sammie's determination would make anyone listen, but would they take us seriously? My mind was flying in so many directions trying to find proof. "The paper said someone called it in. Maybe that was Orson."

"Come on, we gonna have another talking to with the sheriff." Sammie ran out the door.

Following her, I ran right into my spirit guide hovering outside.

"Did I do good?" he asked.

I flashed him a thumbs up as I raced to catch up with Sammie.

48

CURSE IS BROKEN

That little Bender brat and her new friend were running toward the stupid bumbling sheriff. Orson felt the first touch of unease. What did they have up their sleeve?

The three of them talked a few minutes then walked over toward the Legends trailer where the owner was unloading horses. What's going on?

The group seemed to be discussing something. What are they up to?

The girls looked across the grounds, then stopped when they saw me. Why are they staring like that?

The sheriff got on his phone and the others leaned in to listen.

The group walked to my pickup and trailer. Hey that's my truck! Get away from it.

How dare they open my truck door? What are they

looking for?

A gasp involuntarily escaped.

Short ragged inhales.

Light-headed.

Don't hyperventilate.

Control yourself.

The secretary at the Legends Stable answered the phone. It was the boss calling. He was authorizing her to release company records to the sheriff who was on his way over right now.

"Sure. Do you know what he wants? I'll get them ready for him."

"He'll need the phone billing records. Orson's phone is with our business right?"

"Yes it is. I can go right now and pull up the records. But what is it you're looking for?"

"We believe he made a call to the fire department last night and need to verify it. Oh and we just had his truck in for an oil change day before yesterday so you should have access to the recorded mileage on that date. Hand those over to the sheriff too. Thanks."

"You got it." The secretary hung up and searched for the information.

49

LILLIA

Everyone gathered at Kitty's house after an exhausting day. The setting sun threw its glow against Superstition Mountain. Sammie and I were enjoying one last swim in the pool.

Grauntie had told us that company phone records proved Orson made the phone call to the fire department to alert them to the fire. Truck maintenance records showed he drove the extra miles for a trip into town from the trailhead. And that Orson was arrested for arson!

"You were too funny," I told Sammie. "The way you stared down the sheriff and wouldn't take no for an answer."

I ducked as she whipped her arm to splash pool water all over me.

"And what about you Lillia? I kept thinking you'd

shout out that we knew because a ghost told us! But no, you just kept insisting they check the records. You even stomped your feet at them. Pretty dramatic!"

I was still surprised at what we'd accomplished together. "Sometimes drama is called for my friend!"

"You know I'll miss you right?" Sammie said as we hung on the edge of the pool.

"I'll miss you too."

The owner of Legends was even celebrating with us. He assured Matt that they knew nothing about what Orson had been doing to sabotage his business. "And we'll be right here with you to help get the stables running again. There's room for both of us in Apache Junction."

Dorothy and Edgar's grandson Liam joined us. All the writers had been brought back to town early. When Liam learned that Sammie and I had convinced the sheriff to look into Orson as a suspect, and that we even steered him toward clues, he did a great big *yes* fist pump. "I sensed it too. But I'm amazed how you two put it all together. I've been working on a book set on an island. Maybe I can lean on you to give me a few tips about solving mysteries?"

Dorothy said, "That sounds interesting Liam. I'll bet you're talking about Mackinac Island."

Edgar leaned down toward Sammie and me. "Mackinac the Mysterious! It just so happens that is the location of our summer cottage. You are welcome anytime you'd like to come."

Grauntie said, "I've always wanted to tour that island. They only allow horses and bikes for transportation, no cars."

"That's right," Liam said.

"And that one is a fudge nut!" Grauntie said, pointing at me.

"Perfect place for her. Last count we had fourteen fudge shops!" Dorothy said.

Sheriff Barney told Laura, "I'm so grateful to your daughter and her friend for persisting in convincing me to check out Orson."

Laura said, "Thankfully Sammie can be stubborn! We were sorry to hear that someone we knew did this. It's hard to believe still."

Grauntie said, "And he seemed like such a nice man, but looking back it was all to weasel his way in for information. Enough of that. Tonight is for celebrating!"

Dorothy lifted her glass and shouted, "Cheers!"

"That's right, cheers," Matt said. "To all the wonderful friends and neighbors who are supporting us through this. Thank you so very much."

"Will Karen be here soon? She should celebrate with us," Edgar said.

"She's visiting Bones in the hospital. That's still a concern for us. He isn't doing well. Barney visited him just this afternoon. He's in rough shape," Matt said.

But when Karen arrived, she was all smiles. "Our prayers have been answered. Bones has turned the corner and will make it. I can't wait to tell him that the arsonist is caught."

"That's wonderful news," Sheriff Barney said. "Bones will be relieved. He seemed to know more than he could tell me this afternoon."

"His family will fly into Phoenix tomorrow. I called Kitty and she said they could stay here since you and Lillia are leaving early in the morning," Karen said.

"You all have made us feel so welcome." Grauntie gave Karen a hug. "We'll never forget our time here."

In front of everyone Karen walked over to her son and looked up at him. "I feel awful that I doubted you for even a moment. I felt that the old mountain's curse was falling on my family again. And I felt helpless. Like I was just a bystander watching it happen. Matt, can you ever forgive me?"

Matt extended open arms. "But you know the curse is just a legend. It's not real."

"Now I know," she said.

Sammie leaned over and whispered, "I think it's real, but we broke it! With a little help."

I agreed with her.

The End

ABOUT THE AUTHOR AND HER BOOKS...

Brenda Felber enjoys weaving mystery stories with threads of paranormal and history in her middle-grade Pameroy Mystery Series. She hopes you find the stories engaging and inspiring. Each book in the series is set in a different state...only forty-two more to go!

Reviews of *Broken Curse, A Pameroy Mystery in Arizona* are appreciated. They are guideposts for other readers to find books they might enjoy.

Please visit www.pameroymystery.com for further information on the series, along with wonderful images that inspired scenes in the Pameroy Mystery Series books.

facebook.com/brendafelberauthor

instagram.com/brendafelber

BOOKS IN THE SERIES...

PAMEROY MYSTERY SERIES

Made in the USA
Middletown, DE
24 November 2019